OXFORD BOOKWORMS LIBRARY
Human Interest

Jeeves and Friends

SHORT STORIES

Stage 5 (1800 headwords)

Series Editor: Jennifer Bassett
Founder Editor: Tricia Hedge
Activities Editors: Jennifer Bassett and Christine Lindop

P. G. WODEHOUSE

Jeeves and Friends

SHORT STORIES

Retold by
Clare West

OXFORD UNIVERSITY PRESS
2000

Oxford University Press
Great Clarendon Street, Oxford OX2 6DP

Oxford New York

Athens Auckland Bangkok Bogotá Buenos Aires Calcutta Cape Town
Chennai Dar es Salaam Delhi Florence Hong Kong Istanbul Karachi
Kuala Lumpur Madrid Melbourne Mexico City Mumbai Nairobi
Paris São Paulo Shanghai Singapore Taipei Tokyo Toronto Warsaw
and associated companies in
Berlin Ibadan

OXFORD and OXFORD ENGLISH
are trade marks of Oxford University Press

ISBN 0 19 423070 8

Illustrated by Elizabeth-Ann McCorquodale

Printed in Spain

CONTENTS

Jeeves Takes Charge

Now, this business of old Jeeves – my valet, you know – well, a lot of people, like my Aunt Agatha, think I'm much too dependent on him. And what I say is, why not? The man's super-intelligent. I stopped trying to organize my own life a week after he came to work for me. That was about six years ago, just after the rather rummy business of Florence Craye, my Uncle Willoughby's book, and Edwin, the boy scout.

The thing really began when I got back to Easeby, my uncle's country home in Shropshire. I was spending a week or so there, as I usually did in summer, but I had had to break my visit to come back to London, in order to get a new valet. At Easeby I had found Meadowes, my valet at the time, stealing my silk socks. Well, no strong-minded employer should ever put up with that kind of thing. And as I discovered he had stolen a lot of other things here and there, I was forced to sack him and go to London to an employment agency. They sent me Jeeves.

I shall always remember the morning he came. I had been present at a rather cheerful little supper the night before, and consequently was feeling a bit unwell. On top of this, I was trying to read a book Florence Craye had given me. She had been staying at Easeby, and two or three days earlier we had got engaged. I knew she would expect me to finish the book by the time I returned. You see, she was concentrating on developing my intelligence, so that I could understand the kind of thing she was interested in. She was a girl with a wonderful profile, but also a deep sense of serious purpose. You'll see what I mean when I tell you that the book she'd given me to read was called *Behavioural Types of Transactional Thinking*. When I picked it up, it fell open at a page beginning:

> The common understanding involved in most types of human expression is certainly extraordinarily efficient in assisting language, which is its tool, and in producing communication in multi-level society, which is the purpose of both.

All perfectly true, no doubt, but not the kind of thing to throw at a fellow with a morning headache.

I was doing my best to read this bright little book when the bell rang. Painfully, I felt my way to the door and opened it. A polite kind of chappie stood outside.

'I understand that you wish to employ a valet,' he said.

What I really wished to do was die, but I told him to stagger in, and he floated noiselessly through the doorway. I found this rather encouraging, as Meadowes had had flat feet, and used to walk very heavily. This fellow didn't appear to have any feet at all. And he had a serious, sympathetic face. He seemed to understand exactly how I felt.

'Excuse me, sir,' he said gently. Then he disappeared into the kitchen, and came back a moment later with a glass full of cloudy liquid. 'Would you drink this, sir,' he said, very much like a royal doctor taking charge of a sick prince. 'It's my own mixture. Gentlemen have told me they find it most helpful after a late evening.'

I did not care what it was. I was so desperate that I would have drunk anything that offered me a chance of feeling normal again. I swallowed the liquid. At first a bomb seemed to go off inside my head, with flames licking at my throat, and then suddenly everything was all right again. The sun was shining, the birds were singing, and generally speaking, there was life and hope once more.

'You've got the job!' I said, as soon as I could speak. It was clear that this fellow was one of the world's workers, the kind of man every home should have.

'Thank you, sir. My name is Jeeves.'

'Can you start at once?'

'Immediately, sir.'

'Because I have to go down to Easeby, in Shropshire, the day after tomorrow.'

'Very good, sir.' He looked past me at a photo on the piano. 'That is an excellent photograph of Lady Florence Craye, sir. I was at one time employed by her father, Lord Worplesdon. I am afraid I left his employment because I was unable to put up with his unusual habit of wearing evening trousers, a sports shirt and a shooting jacket at dinner.'

Jeeves couldn't tell me anything I didn't know about the old boy's strange ways. I had known the family since I was a kid, and from boyhood I had lived in fear of this man. I shall never forget the time he found me smoking one of his special cigars in his study. I was only fifteen at the time, and smoking was a new experience for me. Just as I was beginning to realize that what I wanted most in the world was a quiet place to lie down, old Worplesdon took his stick and chased me for more than a kilometre across difficult country. I was, of course, absolutely delighted to be engaged to Florence, but if there was a tiny disadvantage, it was that she rather took after her father. She had a wonderful profile, though.

'Lady Florence and I are engaged, Jeeves,' I said.

'Indeed, sir?'

You know, there was a kind of rummy something about his manner. It somehow made me think he didn't like Florence much. Well, of course, it wasn't my business. I supposed that, while he was old Worplesdon's valet, she had probably wounded his feelings by ordering him around. Florence was a dear girl, and seen sideways, awfully good-looking, but if she had a fault, it was that she did not consider politeness necessary when speaking to the servants.

Just then, the door bell rang, and Jeeves floated off to answer it. He came back with a telegram. I opened it and read:

RETURN AT ONCE. EXTREMELY URGENT. CATCH FIRST TRAIN. FLORENCE.

'How odd!' I said.

'Sir?' said Jeeves.

'Oh, nothing,' I replied. It shows how little I knew Jeeves in those days that I didn't go a bit deeper into the matter with him. Now, I would never dream of reading a rummy telegram without asking him what he thought of it. And this one was certainly odd. Florence knew I was going back to Easeby the day after tomorrow, anyway, so why the hurry?

'Jeeves,' I said, 'we shall travel down to Easeby this afternoon. Can you manage the packing and so on by then?'

'Without any difficulty, sir. Which suit will you wear for the journey?'

'This one.' I was wearing a rather cheerful young check suit, which I was extremely fond of. It was perhaps rather sudden until you got used to it, but several of the chaps at my club had shown a lot of interest in it.

'Very good, sir.' Again there was that kind of rummy something in his manner. It was the way he said it. He didn't like the suit. Something seemed to tell me that unless I showed him very soon who was boss, he would take charge and start giving *me* the orders. Well, I wasn't going to put up with that, by Jove! I'd seen so many cases of fellows simply *governed* by their valets. I remember poor Aubrey Fothergill telling me one

'What's wrong with this suit, Jeeves?' I asked coldly.

night – with absolute tears in his eyes, poor chap! – that he had had to give away a pair of brown shoes just because his man didn't like them. I couldn't let that happen to me.

'What's wrong with this suit, Jeeves?' I asked coldly.

'May I suggest, sir, a simple brown or blue—'

'What absolute nonsense! Perfectly silly, my dear man!'

'As you say, sir.'

I was ready to argue, but there didn't seem to be anything to argue about. 'All right, then,' I said.

'Yes, sir.' And he went away to pack the bags, while I started *Behavioural Types of Transactional Thinking* again.

That afternoon, as we travelled down in the train, I was wondering what had happened at Easeby. I didn't think it could be anything very exciting. The house-guests there were all quiet, reasonable people like me. And my uncle wouldn't let anything unusual happen in his house. He was a rather stiff, careful old boy, who liked a peaceful life. For the last year he had been writing a history of the family, which he had nearly finished. People said that when he was young he'd been rather wild, but you'd never guess that if you looked at him now.

When we arrived at the house, Florence came to meet me in the smoking-room. I soon saw that she was annoyed.

'My dearest girl!' I said, and attempted a kiss, but she stepped quickly sideways and said sharply, 'Don't!'

'What's the matter?' I asked.

'Everything's the matter! Bertie, you remember asking me, before you left, to be pleasant to your uncle?' I certainly did remember. As I was more or less dependent on Uncle Willoughby, I couldn't really marry without his agreement. 'You told me it would please him particularly if I asked him to read me some of his history of the family.'

'*Wasn't* he pleased?'

'He was delighted. He finished writing the thing yesterday, and read me nearly all of it last night. I've never had such a shock in my life! The book is horrible!'

'But surely the family weren't as bad as all that!'

'It's not a history of the family at all. He has written his reminiscences! He calls them *Memories of a Long Life*!'

I began to understand. As I said, Uncle Willoughby had led a rather exciting life as a young man, and his memories of it would probably be extremely interesting, even shocking.

'Right at the beginning,' continued Florence, 'there is a story about him and my father which I simply cannot believe. One night in 1887 they were thrown out of a music-hall.'

'Why? I thought you could do almost anything in a music-hall in 1887.'

'I refuse to tell you why – the details are too awful. It appears they had been drinking. The book is full of stories like that. There is an awful one about Lord Emsworth.'

'Lord Emsworth? Not the one we know? At Blandings?'

'That's the one. It seems that he – but I can't tell you!'

'Oh, go on. Try!'

'No! Bertie, the book is unspeakable. And father appears in nearly every story! I am horrified at the things he did when he was a young man. Now listen, your uncle is sending the book off to his publisher in London tomorrow. It must be destroyed before it reaches London!'

I sat up. This sounded rather good fun. 'How are you going to do it?' I asked, interested.

'How can I do it? I am going to a house-party tonight and

shall not be back till Monday. *You* must do it. That is why I sent you the telegram.'

'What!'

She gave me a look. 'Do you mean to say you refuse to help me, Bertie?'

'No, but – I say! You know – I mean—'

'It's quite simple. You say you want to marry me, Bertie?'

'Yes, of course, but still—'

For a moment she looked exactly like her old father. 'I will never marry you if those reminiscences are published.'

'But, Florence, old thing!'

'I mean it, Bertie. This is a kind of test. If you succeed, it will prove you are not the foolish, useless person most people think you are. If you fail, I shall know that your Aunt Agatha was right when she advised me strongly not to marry you.'

'But suppose Uncle Willoughby catches me stealing his book? He won't leave me any of his money when he dies!'

'If you care more for your uncle's money than for me—'

'No, no! Absolutely not!'

'Very well, then. The parcel containing the book will be placed on the hall table tomorrow, for the servants to post. All you have to do is take it and destroy it!'

'But – but – but—' I could think of hundreds of reasons why this would not be a good plan.

'Bertie, will you or will you not do this small thing for me? If not, say so now and stop pretending you care for me!'

'Dear old thing, of course I love you!'

'Then will you or will you not—'

'Oh, all right,' I said. 'All right! All right! All right!' And I staggered out to think about it.

I've often wondered since then how these murderer fellows manage to keep in condition while planning their next crime. I had a much simpler job than murder to do, and I give you my word, I couldn't sleep at all that night.

All the next day I waited in or near the hall, feeling like a thief at a railway station. I did not dare imagine what Uncle Willoughby would say if he caught me stealing the parcel. As I say, he was normally a quiet man, but, by Jove, this kind of thing was likely to make him very angry indeed.

It wasn't until about four in the afternoon that he put the parcel on the hall table and went back into his study. I rushed over, took it, and ran upstairs to my bedroom. Throwing open the door, I was horrified to see young Edwin, the boy scout, re-arranging my ties in a drawer. This awful kid was Florence's young brother, who was spending his school holiday at Easeby. He had recently joined the boy scouts, and took his duties very seriously. You may know that a scout has to do an act of kindness to someone every day. Nasty little Edwin rarely managed this, so sometimes he had to do several acts of kindness in one day, to catch up. His idea of kindness was not the same as anyone else's, and this made life perfectly horrible for everyone at Easeby, I can tell you.

'What are you doing here?' I asked.

'I'm making your room tidy. It's my last Saturday's act of kindness.'

It became more and more obvious to me that this unpleasant kid must be removed as soon as possible. I had the parcel behind my back, and I hoped he hadn't seen it, but I was desperate to hide it somewhere.

'Don't bother about tidying the room,' I said.

'I like tidying it. It's no trouble.'

This was becoming perfectly awful. I didn't want to murder the kid, and there seemed no other way of getting rid of him. Suddenly I had an idea.

'There's something much kinder you could do. Take that box of cigars down to the smoking-room, and cut the ends off for me. That would be really helpful. Stagger along, my boy.'

He looked a bit doubtful, but he staggered. I threw the parcel into a drawer, locked it, and put the key in my pocket, feeling better immediately. I went downstairs, and as I passed the smoking-room, Edwin ran out. It seemed to me that if he wanted to do a real act of kindness, he would kill himself.

'I'm cutting them,' he said.

'Carry on! Carry on!'

'Do you like them cut a lot or a little?'

'Medium.'

'All right. I'll carry on, then.'

'That's it!' And we separated.

Fellows who know all about crime will tell you that the most difficult thing in the world is to get rid of the body. Florence had told me to destroy the parcel, but how could I? I couldn't burn it, because people would suspect something if I asked for a fire in my room in the middle of summer. And I couldn't eat it, like a chap with a secret message on the battlefield, because it would take me about a year. So I just left it in the drawer, and worried about it. It made me feel so guilty that I jumped every time anyone spoke to me.

Early on Friday evening, Uncle Willoughby asked for a private word with me. He was looking considerably annoyed.

'Bertie, an extremely worrying thing has happened. As you

know, I sent my book to the publishers yesterday. It should have arrived this morning. But when I telephoned them just now, they informed me they had not yet received it.'

'Very rummy!'

'I remember placing it on the hall table yesterday. But here is the strange thing. It seems that it was not there when the servants collected the letters for posting.'

'Sounds odd!'

'Bertie, you may not believe this, but I suspect that someone has stolen the parcel.'

'Oh, I say! Surely not!'

'Listen. It is a fact that during the last few weeks a number of things have disappeared from the house, and—'

'But, uncle, one moment. It was my man Meadowes who stole all those things. He was stealing my socks, too. Caught him actually doing it, by Jove!'

'Really, Bertie? Send for him at once and question him!'

'But he isn't here. You see, I sacked him. That's why I went to London – to get a new valet.'

'So if your man Meadowes is no longer in the house, he cannot be the thief. There seems to be no explanation.'

We sat together silently for a while, but soon my guilty secret hung so heavily on me that I went out for a cigarette and a breath of fresh air. It was one of those peaceful summer evenings when you can hear a sheep chewing a mile away, and I was just beginning to feel calmer, when suddenly I heard my name spoken.

'It's about Bertie.' It was the hateful voice of young Edwin, inside the house! I looked around and saw that the open window of my uncle's study was just behind me. I threw my cigarette

11

It was the hateful voice of young Edwin, inside the house!

away and hid behind a bush under the open window, to listen
to the conversation. I knew something terrible was about to
happen.

'About Bertie?' I heard Uncle Willoughby say.

'About Bertie and your parcel. I believe he's got it. I saw him
go into his room yesterday with a parcel behind his back. And
when he came downstairs again, he wasn't carrying it.'

They deliberately teach these nasty little scouts to notice
things, you know. Just look at the trouble it causes.

'But why would Bertie do that?' asked Uncle Willoughby.

'Perhaps it was Bertie who stole all those things from the
beginning. But I'm sure he's got the parcel. I know! You could
say that a guest who stayed in Bertie's room recently has asked
you to look for something he left there. Then you could search
Bertie's room.'

I didn't wait to hear any more. Things were getting too hot.
I ran into the house, and straight upstairs to my room. And then
I realized I couldn't find the key to the drawer anywhere.

Just then I heard a footstep outside, and in came Uncle
Willoughby. 'Oh, Bertie,' he said calmly, 'I have – ah – just
received a telegram from a previous guest, Mr Berkeley, who
thinks he may have left a – ah – cigarette case in this room.'

It was horrifying to see this white-haired old man lying to
me like an actor. 'I haven't seen it anywhere,' I said.

'I think I will search for it anyway. Perhaps it is in one of
these drawers.' He pulled out drawer after drawer. I just stood
there, feeling weaker every moment. Then he came to the
drawer where the parcel was. 'This one appears to be locked,'
he said. 'Have you the key?'

A soft voice spoke behind me. 'I imagine, sir, that this is the key you need. It was in the pocket of these trousers.' It was Jeeves. He had floated in, carrying the trousers, and was holding out the key. I could have murdered him.

The next moment Uncle Willoughby had opened the drawer. I shut my eyes. 'No,' he said, 'nothing here. Thank you, Bertie. I am sorry if I have disturbed you.'

When he had gone, I closed the door carefully and turned to Jeeves. It was difficult to know how to begin.

'Jeeves, did you – was there – have you, by any chance—'

'I removed the parcel this morning, sir.'

'I suppose this all seems rather rummy to you, Jeeves?'

'Not at all, sir. I happened to hear you and Lady Florence speaking of the matter the other evening, sir.'

'Did you, by Jove? Well – er – Jeeves, I think it would be better if you could hold on to the parcel – until we get back to London – er – and then – you know – destroy it.'

'I quite understand, sir. Leave it to me, sir.'

'You know, Jeeves, you're one in a million. One in a million, by Jove!'

'It is very kind of you to say so, sir.'

'Well, that's about all, then, I think.'

'Very good, sir.'

When Florence returned on Monday, she asked me at once, 'Well, Bertie? Have you destroyed the book?'

'Not exactly,' I said, 'but it's all right.'

'Bertie, what do you mean?' she asked sharply. I was just going to explain, when Uncle Willoughby came running happily out of his study like a two-year-old.

'A most surprising thing, Bertie! My publisher has just

telephoned to say he has received my book. There must have been some delay in our very inefficient postal service.'

I was looking at Florence's profile as he spoke, and at that moment she turned round and gave me a look that went through me like a knife. Uncle Willoughby returned to his study, and there was a heavy silence.

'I can't understand it, by Jove!' I said at last.

'*I* can. I can understand it perfectly, Bertie. Rather than risk offending your uncle, you—'

'No, no! Absolutely not!'

'You preferred to lose me rather than risk losing your inheritance. I meant what I said. Our engagement is over.'

'But, I say, Florence, old thing!'

'Not another word. I do not wish to hear any more. I see now that your Aunt Agatha was perfectly right. There was a time when I thought I could, with patience, make you into something, but that is clearly impossible. Goodbye!'

And she departed, leaving me to pick up the pieces. I went to my room and rang for Jeeves. He appeared.

'Jeeves!' I shouted. 'That parcel has arrived in London!'

'Yes, sir. I sent it, sir. I considered that you and Lady Florence were wrong in thinking that people would be offended by Sir Willoughby's book. When my aunt published—'

'Forget about your aunt, Jeeves! Do you know Lady Florence has broken off our engagement?'

'Indeed, sir?' He didn't appear the least bit sympathetic.

'You're sacked!'

'Very good, sir.' After a moment, he said, 'As I am no longer in your employment, sir, I can speak freely. In my opinion you and Lady Florence would not have been happy together. Lady

Florence's character is so different from yours.'

'Get out!'

'I think you would also have found her continual attempts to educate you a little annoying, sir. The book she gave you to read is most unsuitable, sir, and I understand, from a conversation Lady Florence was having with another guest, that she was planning to start you on Nietzsche very soon. You would not enjoy Nietzsche, sir. An extremely difficult writer.'

'Get out!'

'Very good, sir.'

It's rummy how things often seem quite different the next day. Somehow, when I woke up next morning, the old heart didn't feel half as broken as it had done. It was a perfectly beautiful day, with the birds singing and all that, which made me wonder if perhaps Jeeves was right after all. Even though she had a wonderful profile, was it such a great idea being engaged to Florence? I began to think my dream wife was rather different, quite a bit more loving and sensitive and so on.

I had thought as far as this when *Behavioural Types of Transactional Thinking* caught my eye. I opened it, and I give you my honest word, this is what hit me:

> Of the two ancient systems of political thinking, one only was real and self-controlling; the other, irregular and imperfect, was considered unreal and, as a result, made sense only by including self-evident truths appearing through.

Well – I ask you! And Nietzsche, according to Jeeves, is a lot worse than that!

'Jeeves,' I said, when he came in with my morning tea, 'I've been thinking. You've got your job back.'

'Thank you, sir.'

I drank a cheerful mouthful, and began to realize this chap knew a thing or two. 'Oh, Jeeves,' I said, 'about that check suit. Is it really awful?'

'A little too loud, sir, in my opinion.'

'But lots of fellows have asked who made it for me.'

'Doubtless in order to avoid him, sir.'

I hesitated a bit. I had a feeling that if I gave in now, I would never take charge again. On the other hand, this was obviously a chap of unusual intelligence, and it seemed sensible to let him do the thinking for me. 'All right, Jeeves,' I said. 'Give the thing away to someone!'

He looked down at me like a father forgiving a child who has done wrong. 'Thank you, sir. I gave it to the under-gardener last night. A little more tea, sir?'

The Artistic Career of Corky

You may notice, as you read these reminiscences of mine, that from time to time things happen in and around the city of New York. It is just possible that this may cause you to look surprised, and ask yourselves, 'What is Bertram doing so far from England, the land he loves so well?'

Well, to cut a longish story short, what happened was that my Aunt Agatha once sent me over to America. My orders were to try to stop young Gussie, my cousin, marrying a girl who was an actress. I managed the whole thing so badly that I decided I had better stay in New York instead of going back and having long cosy conversations with Aunt Agatha about it.

So I sent Jeeves out to find a reasonable flat, and made myself as comfortable as I could, for a long stay. I must say, New York is a most cheerful place to live in, if things are too hot for you at home. Fellows introduced me to other fellows and so on, and it wasn't long before I knew large numbers of the right sort. Some of them – the wealthy types – lived in big houses up by Central Park, and others – the not-so-wealthy artists and writers and so on – lived mostly around Washington Square.

Corky, whose real name was Bruce Corcoran, was one of the artists. A portrait-painter, he called himself, but in fact his score up to now had been zero. You see, the difficulty about portrait-painting – I've looked into the thing a bit – is that you can't start painting portraits until people come along and ask you to, and they won't come and ask you until you've painted a lot first. This makes it kind of difficult, not to say tough, for the ambitious young man.

Corky managed to make a little money by drawing an occasional funny picture for the newspapers – he could produce something quite amusing when he got a good idea. But his main income came from his rich uncle, Alexander Worple, who was in the jute business. I'm not quite sure what jute is, exactly, but it seems that people are very keen on it, because Mr Worple had made a huge fortune out of selling it.

Now, a lot of fellows think that having a rich uncle makes life easy, but Corky tells me this is not true. Worple was only fifty-one, a strong, healthy sort of chap, who looked capable of living for ever. It was not this, however, that worried poor Corky, who did not mind his uncle going on living. What really annoyed Corky was the way old Worple used to bother him constantly. Corky's uncle, you see, didn't want him to be an artist. He didn't think Corky was good enough. He was always trying to persuade him to give up Art and go into the jute business, starting at the bottom and working up. But Corky said that, although he didn't know what people did at the bottom of the jute business, he felt sure it was something too horrible for words. He believed in his future as an artist, and wanted to make a career of Art. Meanwhile, his uncle, rather unwillingly, paid him a small allowance four times a year.

Corky wouldn't even have received this if his uncle hadn't had a hobby. In his spare time Mr Worple studied birds. He had written a book called *American Birds*, and was writing another, which would be called *More American Birds*. When he had finished that one, he was expected to begin a third, and go on until there were no more American birds left. Corky used to visit him once every three months, and just sat there, while his uncle talked about birds. As long as Corky listened politely for an hour or so, he felt more or less sure he would receive his allowance. But it was rather unpleasant for the poor chap. He never really *knew* for certain if he would get the money, you see, and anyway, he was only interested in birds served on a dish, with a good bottle of cold dry white wine.

Mr Worple was a man of extremely uncertain temper. He also seemed to think that Corky was a poor fool who could not manage anything successfully. I expect Jeeves feels very much the same about me. So when Corky staggered into my apartment one afternoon, pushing a girl gently in front of him, and said, 'Bertie, I want you to meet my fiancée, Miss Singer,' I immediately realized what his problem was.

'Corky, what about your uncle?' I asked. The poor chap gave a shaky laugh.

'We're so worried,' said the girl. 'We were hoping you could suggest a way of breaking the news gently to Mr Worple.'

Muriel Singer was one of those quiet, good-looking girls, who have a way of looking at you with their big eyes. 'You are the greatest thing on earth,' they seem to say. 'You big strong man, you!' She gave a fellow a wonderful feeling, made him want to take her hand and say, 'Don't worry, little one!' or something like that. What I mean is, she made me feel brave and clever and capable, all at the same time.

'I should think your uncle would be delighted to hear you're engaged,' I said to Corky. 'He'll consider Miss Singer the perfect wife for you.'

Corky didn't look any happier. 'You don't know him. He's got a very strange character. If he liked Muriel, he'd still pretend he didn't. If I tell him I'm engaged, he'll just think I've decided something important without asking him, and he'll automatically lose his temper. He's always done that.'

My brain was working overtime to meet this emergency. 'You want to arrange for him to meet Miss Singer without knowing that you know her. Then you come along—'

'But how can I arrange that?'

I saw his point. That was the difficulty. 'There's only one thing to do,' I said.

'What's that?'

'Leave it to Jeeves.' And I rang the bell.

'Sir?' said Jeeves, appearing from nowhere. One of the rummy things about Jeeves is that, unless you watch him closely, you rarely see him come into a room. He's like one of those strange chaps in India who can disappear into thin air and then reappear in another place.

The moment I saw him standing there, listening politely, I felt hugely relieved, like a lost child who sees his father in the distance. 'Jeeves,' I said, 'we want your advice.'

'Very good, sir.'

I told him Corky's painful story in a few well-chosen words. 'So you see the problem, Jeeves. How can Mr Worple get to know Miss Singer, without realizing that Mr Corcoran already knows her? Can you try to think of something?'

'I have thought of something already, sir.'

'You have, by Jove!'

'My plan is certain to succeed, sir, but I am afraid the costs will be considerable.'

This made poor Corky look depressed. But I was still under the influence of the girl's melting look, and I saw that I could help. 'Don't worry about that, Corky,' I said. 'I'll be only too glad to be of assistance. Carry on, Jeeves.'

21

'I suggest, sir, that Mr Corcoran should take advantage of the fact that Mr Worple is so fond of birds. The young lady could write a small book, called, for example, *The Children's Book of American Birds*. All the way through the work there

'Jeeves,' I said, 'we want your advice.'

would be frequent and enthusiastic remarks about Mr Worple's own book on birds. You, sir, would pay to have a limited number of copies of this book published. Then we would send a copy to Mr Worple, with a letter from the young lady, in which she asks to meet the author to whom she owes so much. This, I imagine, would produce the result you wish for.'

I felt extremely proud of Jeeves. What a brain that man has!

'Jeeves,' I said, 'that is absolutely wonderful. One of your very best ideas.'

'Thank you, sir.'

The girl said, 'But I couldn't write a book about anything. I can't even write good letters.'

'You see, Bertie,' said Corky, 'Muriel is more of a dancer and a singer, than a writer. In fact, she's appearing in *Choose your Exit* at the Manhattan Theatre. I didn't mention it before, but that's why we feel a little worried about how Uncle Alexander will receive the news. He's so unreasonable!'

But Jeeves had the answer, of course. 'I imagine it would be a simple matter, sir, to find some author in need of money who would be glad to do the actual writing.'

'That's true,' said Corky. 'Sam Patterson would do it for a hundred dollars. I'll get in touch with him at once.'

'Fine!' I said.

'Will that be all, sir?' said Jeeves. 'Very good, sir.'

I always used to think that publishers were extremely brainy fellows, but I know better now. All a publisher has to do is write occasional cheques, while a lot of hard-working chappies do the real work. I know, because I've been a publisher myself.

I simply sat in the old flat with a pen and a chequebook, and one day a lovely shiny new book appeared.

The girl's name was written in gold letters on the red cover. I opened it and read:

Often on a spring morning, as you walk through the fields, you will hear the sweet, carelessly-flowing song of the Eastern Bluebird. When you are older, you must read all about him in Mr Alexander Worple's wonderful book, *American Birds*.

You see. And only a few pages later there was another mention of the uncle, connected to the Yellow-headed Blackbird. It was great writing. I didn't see how the uncle could fail to feel warmly towards Miss Singer.

And a day or so later Corky staggered up to my flat to tell me that all was well. Mr Worple had written Muriel a letter so full of the milk of human kindness that Corky almost refused to believe his uncle had written it. Any time it suited Miss Singer to call, said the uncle, he would be delighted to meet her.

Soon after this I had to leave New York, to visit several of my new friends at their country places. So it wasn't until some months later that I came back to the city again. I hadn't heard from Corky, and had been wondering how things had gone in my absence. On my first evening back in New York, I happened to go into a quiet sort of little restaurant, and there, sitting alone at a table, was Muriel Singer. I greeted her.

'Why, Mr Wooster! How are you?' she replied.

'Where's Corky?'

'I beg your pardon?'

'You're waiting for Corky, aren't you?'

'Oh, I didn't understand. No, I'm not waiting for him.'

It seemed to me there was a sort of something in her voice. 'I say, you and Corky haven't been arguing, have you?'

'Why, whatever makes you think that?'

'Oh, well, what I mean is – I thought you usually had dinner with him before you went to the theatre.'

'I don't work in the theatre any more.'

Suddenly the whole thing was clear to me. I had forgotten what a long time I had been away. 'Why, of course, I see now! You're married!'

'Yes.'

'How perfectly wonderful! I wish you every happiness.'

'Thank you so much. Oh, Alexander,' she said, looking past me, 'this is a friend of mine – Mr Wooster.' I turned round quickly. A fellow with a lot of stiff grey hair and a red sort of healthy face was standing there. 'I want you to meet my husband, Mr Wooster. This is a friend of Bruce's, Alexander.'

The old boy shook my hand warmly, and that was all that prevented me from falling to the floor.

'So you know my nephew, Mr Wooster?' I heard him say. 'I wish you would try to make him give up this playing at painting. But I think perhaps he's less wild these days. I noticed it that night he came to dinner with us, my dear, when he was first introduced to you. He seemed quieter and more serious than before. Now, Mr Wooster, will you have dinner with us tonight? It would be a pleasure for us.'

I said I had already had dinner, and left. What I needed then was air, not food. When I reached my flat, I called Jeeves.

'Jeeves,' I said, 'this is urgent. A stiff brandy for me, first of

25

all, and you'd better have one yourself. I've got some news that will shock you.'

'I won't have one just now, thank you, sir. Perhaps later.'

'All right. But prepare yourself. You remember Mr Corcoran? And the girl who was supposed to slide smoothly into his uncle's circle of friends, by writing the book on birds?'

'I remember perfectly, sir.'

'Well, she's slid. She's married the uncle.'

He took it without showing any surprise. You can't shock Jeeves. 'That was always a possible development, sir.'

'Really, by Jove! I think you could have warned us.'

'I didn't like to take the liberty, sir.'

Of course, after I had had a bite to eat and was in a calmer mood, I realized that what had happened wasn't my fault. But all the same, I must say I didn't look forward to meeting Corky again until time had lessened his pain a bit. I avoided Washington Square absolutely for the next few months. And then, just when I was beginning to think I could safely stagger in that direction, the most awful thing happened. Opening the paper one morning, I read that Mr and Mrs Alexander Worple had just had a son. I was so dashed sorry for poor old Corky that I hadn't the heart to touch my breakfast. It was the end. Absolutely. He had lost the girl he loved, and now he had lost the Worple jute millions as well!

I wanted, of course, to hurry down to Washington Square and show the poor fellow how sympathetic I felt, but when I thought about it, absence seemed the best medicine. I gave him litres of it.

But after a month or so, I began to realize that the poor chap probably needed his friends even more at a moment like this.

I imagined him sitting in his lonely room with nothing but his bitter thoughts, and this made me so sad that I jumped into a taxi and told the driver to drive there at once.

When I arrived, I found Corky at work. He was painting, while on a chair in the middle of the room sat a cross-looking woman holding a baby.

'Hallo, Bertie,' said Corky. 'We're just finishing for the day. That will be all this afternoon – the same time tomorrow, please,' he told the nurse, who got up with the baby and left.

Corky turned to me and began to pour out his feelings. 'It's my uncle's idea. The portrait will be a surprise for Muriel on her birthday. Just think, Bertie! It's the first time anyone's ever asked me to paint a portrait, and the sitter is that human boiled egg, who's stolen my uncle's fortune from me! Can you believe it! Now I have to spend my afternoons staring into that little kid's ugly face! I can't refuse to paint the portrait, because if I did, my uncle would stop my allowance. But I tell you, Bertie, sometimes when that kid turns and looks unpleasantly at me, I come close to murdering him. There are moments when I can almost see the front page of the evening newspaper: "Promising Young Artist Kills Baby With Hammer".'

I touched his shoulder silently. My sympathy for the poor old fellow was too deep for words.

For some time after that, I kept away from his flat, because it didn't seem right to disturb the poor chappie in his misery. Anyway, that dashed nurse reminded me of Aunt Agatha. She had the same cold stare.

But one afternoon Corky phoned me. 'Bertie, could you come down here this afternoon? I've finished the portrait.'

'Good boy! Great work!'

'Yes.' He sounded doubtful. 'The fact is, Bertie, it doesn't look quite right to me. My uncle's coming in half an hour to inspect it, and – I don't know why, but I feel I'd like your support!'

'You think he'll get nasty?'

'He may.'

I remembered the red-faced chappie I had met in the restaurant. It was only too easy to imagine him getting nasty.

'I'll come,' I told Corky, 'but only if I can bring Jeeves.'

'Why Jeeves? Jeeves was the fool who suggested . . .'

'Listen, Corky, old thing! If you think I'm going to meet that uncle of yours without Jeeves's support, you're wrong! I'd rather go up to a tiger and bite it on the back of the neck.'

'Oh, all right,' said Corky, unwillingly.

So Jeeves and I went round to Corky's flat. We found him looking worriedly at the picture. The light from the big window fell right on the portrait. I took a good look at it, then went closer to examine it. Then I went back to where I had been at first, because it hadn't seemed quite so bad from there.

'Well?' said Corky, anxiously.

I hesitated a bit. 'Of course, old man, I only saw the kid once, but – but it *was* an ugly sort of kid, wasn't it?'

'As ugly as that?'

I looked again, and honesty forced me to be truthful. 'I don't see how it could have been, old chap.'

Poor old Corky looked miserable. 'You're quite right, Bertie. Something's gone wrong with the dashed thing. I think I must have got through the kid's outward appearance, and painted his soul.'

'But he's so young! Could a child of that age have a soul as bad as that? What do you think, Jeeves?'

'I doubt it, sir. The child's expression is most unpleasant, and he has a decidedly inebriated manner, sir.'

Just then the door opened and the uncle came in. For about

'It was an ugly sort of kid, wasn't it?'

three seconds all was sweetness and light. 'Nice to see you, Mr Wooster. How are you, Bruce, my boy? So, the portrait is really finished, is it? Well, bring it out. Let's have a look. This will be a wonderful surprise for your aunt—'

Then he saw it, suddenly, before he was ready. He stepped quickly backwards. For perhaps a minute there was one of the worst silences I've ever experienced.

'Is this a joke?' he asked, turning violently on Corky, like a wild animal that smells red meat. 'You call yourself a painter! I wouldn't let you paint a house of mine! I asked you to paint a portrait, and this – this – this is the result! Well, let me tell you something. Unless you come to my office on Monday, prepared to give up all these stupid ideas and ready to start at the bottom of the business, I won't give you another cent – not another cent!' The door opened and closed behind him.

'Corky, old man!' I whispered sympathetically.

'Well, that finishes it,' said Corky in a broken voice. 'What can I do? I can't keep on painting if he cuts off my allowance. You heard what he said. I'll have to go to the office on Monday.'

I couldn't think of a thing to say. I knew exactly how he felt about the office – it would be like going to prison.

And then a calm voice broke the silence.

'If I could suggest something, sir?'

It was Jeeves. He had slid from the shadows and was looking seriously at the portrait. 'It seems to me, sir, that if Mr Corcoran looks into the matter, he will find a way of solving the problem. The picture may not please Mr Worple as a portrait of his only child, but it is fresh and lively, and catches the attention. I have no doubt that newspaper and magazine publishers would pay well for a number of amusing drawings, with this baby as the central character. I feel sure it would be highly popular.'

Corky was staring angrily at the picture. Suddenly he began to laugh wildly and stagger all over the floor. I feared the poor chap had gone mad.

'He's right! Absolutely right! Jeeves, you're a lifesaver! Go to the office on Monday! Start at the bottom of the business! I'll *buy* the business if I feel like it! I know a publisher who'll pay me anything I like for this! Where's my hat? Lend me five dollars, Bertie. I'll take a taxi to Park Row!'

Jeeves smiled in a fatherly way. Or rather, he moved his mouth a bit, which is the nearest he ever gets to smiling.

'May I suggest a name, Mr Corcoran, for these drawings you are planning? "The Adventures of Baby Blobby".'

Corky and I looked at the picture, then at each other. Jeeves was absolutely right. There could be no other name.

A few weeks later, I was having breakfast in bed and smiling at Corky's drawings in *The Sunday Star*.

'You know, Jeeves,' I said, 'you really are wonderful. Look how well Corky's doing, and it's all because of you.'

'I am pleased to say that Mr Corcoran has been most generous to me, sir. I am putting out the brown suit for you, sir.'

'No, I think I'll wear the blue with the thin red stripe.'

'Not the blue with the thin red stripe, sir.'

'But I think it suits me rather well.'

'Not the blue with the thin red stripe, sir.'

'Oh, all right, have it your own way.'

'Very good, sir. Thank you, sir.'

Bertie Changes His Mind
– A story told by Jeeves –

It has happened so frequently in the past that young fellows starting in my profession have come to me for a word of advice, that I have found it convenient to put my answer into a few words. Resource and tact – that is what I advise. Tact, of course, has always been part of my nature, and as for resource, well, I think I may say that I have shown a certain intelligence when solving those little problems that appear from time to time in the daily life of a gentleman's personal gentleman.

I am reminded, for example, of Mr Wooster's visit to the School for Young Ladies near Brighton. The story started one evening, when I brought Mr Wooster his whisky, as I always did. He had been strangely moody for some days – far from his normal cheerful self. I thought he was still suffering from the effects of a recent illness, and, of course, took no notice, carrying out my duties as usual. But on this particular evening, when I brought him his whisky, he spoke to me with remarkable annoyance.

'Oh, dash it, Jeeves!' he said with feeling. 'Couldn't you at least put it on another table for a change?'

'Sir?' I said.

'Every night, dash it,' continued Mr Wooster, frowning, 'you come in at exactly the same time with the same old drinks and put them on the same old table. I've had enough, I tell you. It's the awful sameness of it that makes it seem so – so awful.'

I confess that his words filled me with a certain fear. I had heard some of my previous employers speak in more or less the same way before, and it had almost always meant that they were thinking of marriage. I was worried, therefore, when Mr Wooster spoke to me in this way, as I had no wish to leave such a kind and generous employer. However, my experience is that when the wife comes in at the front door, the valet of bachelor days goes out at the back.

'It's not your fault, of course,' Mr Wooster went on, looking a little calmer. 'I'm not blaming you. But you know, Jeeves, I've been thinking rather deeply these last few days, and I've decided that mine is an empty life. I'm lonely, Jeeves.'

'You have a large number of friends, sir.'

'What's the use of having friends? No, Jeeves, what I want is – have you seen that play called I-forget-its-dashed-name?'

'No, sir.'

'It's on at the What-do-you-call-it Theatre. I went last night. There's a chap in it who's just staggering through life as usual, you know, when suddenly a kid appears and says she's his daughter. Absolutely the first he's ever heard of it. Well, in the end he takes the kid and they go out into the world together, you know. Well, what I'm saying, Jeeves, is that I would have liked to be that chappie. Awfully jolly little girl, you know, very loving and friendly and so on. Something to look after, if you know what I mean. Jeeves, I wish I had a daughter. I wonder how people do it?'

'I believe marriage is considered the first step, sir.'

'No, I mean *adopting* a kid. You can adopt kids, you know, Jeeves. What I want to know is how you start.'

'I should imagine it would be a highly complicated and difficult matter, sir. It would cut into your spare time.'

'Well, I'll tell you what I'll do, then. My sister will be back from India next week with her three little girls. I'll give up this flat and rent a house and have them all to live with me. By Jove, that's rather a good idea, isn't it, Jeeves? The happy sound of childish voices? Little feet running here and there? What do you think?'

I hid my feelings, with some difficulty. Mr Wooster's plan would mean the end of our cosy bachelor arrangements. No doubt some men in my position would have expressed their displeasure at this point, but I avoided making this mistake.

'If you do not mind my saying so, sir, I think you are still a little weak after your recent illness. If I might offer an opinion, what you need is a few days by the sea. Brighton is near, sir.'

'Are you suggesting that I've gone a bit crazy?'

'Certainly not, sir. It is only that I think a short stay in Brighton would be extremely good for your health.'

Mr Wooster considered. 'Well, I'm not sure you're not right,' he said at last. 'I *am* feeling a bit low. You could throw a few things in a case and drive me down there tomorrow.'

'Very good, sir.'

'And when we get back, I'll be bursting with health and ready to start on this plan of mine.'

'Exactly, sir.'

Well, the situation was safe for the moment, but I began to realize that this was going to be a serious problem. I had rarely seen Mr Wooster more determined. Perhaps the last time he had shown such firmness was when he insisted, against my clearly expressed advice, on wearing purple socks. However, that crisis had passed, and I did not lack confidence in my ability to solve the present problem just as successfully. Employers are like horses. They need managing. Some gentlemen's personal gentlemen know how to manage them, some do not. I, I am happy to say, have no reason to complain.

For myself, I found our stay in Brighton highly enjoyable, but Mr Wooster was still restless, and became tired of the place within two days. So on the third afternoon he ordered me to pack the bags and drive him back to London. We started back along the main road at about five on a fine summer's day, and had travelled about three kilometres, when I saw a young lady in the road, waving at us. I stopped the car, and the girl ran towards us.

'I expect she wants a lift, Jeeves,' said Mr Wooster. 'A jolly-looking kid. I wonder what she's doing, out on the main road.'

'She has the appearance, sir, of someone who is absent from school without permission.'

'Hallo-allo-allo!' said Mr Wooster, as the child reached us. 'Can we give you a lift?'

'Oh, I say, can you?' said the child delightedly. 'My school's just down the road, on the left. If you put me down in another kilometre or so, I'll walk the rest of the way. I say, thanks awfully.'

She climbed in. A red-haired young person with a small, flat nose and an extremely cheerful smile. Her age, I should imagine, would be about twelve.

'I'm going to get into terrible trouble,' she went on. 'Miss Tomlinson will be awfully angry.'

'No, really?' said Mr Wooster, sympathetically.

'You see, they gave us a half day's holiday today, so I went out of the school while nobody was looking, and spent the afternoon in Brighton. It's rather fun there! I thought I could

35

get back in time for tea, so that nobody would notice I'd gone, but now I'm late, and they'll all be angry with me, because of course we're not allowed to leave the school without permission.'

Mr Wooster was visibly upset. 'Oh, I say, this is awful,' he remarked. 'Jeeves, don't you think we could do something?'

'I imagine so, yes, sir. I think you might inform the young lady's headmistress that you are an old friend of the young lady's father. You could mention that you were passing the school, when you saw the young lady at the gate, and took her for a drive. When Miss Tomlinson hears this, she will no doubt be considerably less angry. She may even express no annoyance at all.'

'Well, you *are* clever!' said the young person. And then she kissed me. I am sorry to say she had just been eating some sugary kind of sweet.

'Jeeves, you've got it!' said Mr Wooster. 'A great plan.' He turned to the child. 'I say, I suppose I'd better know your name, if I'm a friend of your father's.'

'My name's Peggy Mainwaring. And my father's Professor Mainwaring. He's written a lot of books.'

'Author of the well-known books on the history of thought, sir,' I mentioned. 'Shall I drive on to the school, sir?'

'Yes, carry on. I say, Jeeves, it's a strange thing. Do you know, I've never been inside a girls' school in my life?'

'Indeed, sir?'

'Ought to be a dashed interesting experience, Jeeves, don't you think?'

'I imagine that you may find it so, sir.'

We drove on down the road, turned in through the gates of

'Well, you are clever!' said the young person.

a large, rather grand building, and parked in front of the main
entrance. Mr Wooster and child entered the school, and soon
a servant came out to speak to me.

'Would you take the car round to the garage, please,' she
said. 'Miss Peggy has taken the gentleman to meet her friends.
And the cook says she hopes you'll come to the kitchen to have
a cup of tea.'

'Inform her I shall be delighted. But first, would it be possible
for me to have a word with Miss Tomlinson?'

A moment later I was following her into the headmistress's
study.

Handsome but firm – that is how I would describe Miss
Tomlinson. In some ways she reminded me of Mr Wooster's
Aunt Agatha, with the same cool stare and the same obvious
unwillingness to put up with any nonsense.

'I fear that I am possibly taking a liberty, madam,' I began, 'but I am hoping you will allow me to say a word about my employer. When he informed you that he was a friend of Professor Mainwaring's, he perhaps did not inform you that he was *the* Mr Wooster.'

'*The* Mr Wooster?'

'Bertram Wooster, madam.'

I will say for Mr Wooster that, however short of intelligence he is, he has a name that suggests almost unlimited possibilities. He sounds like Someone, especially if you have been told he is a close friend of the famous Professor Mainwaring. As I had rather expected, Miss Tomlinson clearly did not want to show how little she knew about him, and so she smiled brightly.

'Oh, *Bertram* Wooster!' she said.

'He is an extremely modest gentleman, and would be the last to suggest it himself, madam, but knowing him as I do, I am sure he would be only too happy to give a talk to the young ladies. He is an excellent speaker.'

'A very good idea,' said Miss Tomlinson decidedly. 'Thank you for suggesting it. I will certainly ask him to talk to the girls.'

'And if he pretends – through modesty – that he doesn't wish to—'

'I shall insist.'

'Thank you, madam. You will not mention our little conversation? Mr Wooster might think this was not part of my duties.'

I drove the car round to the garage. It was a good car, and appeared to be in excellent condition. But somehow I had the feeling something was going to go wrong with it – something serious – something that I could not repair for at least a couple of hours.

About half an hour later Mr Wooster came to the back of the house to find me. I noticed that he seemed a little tired, and his eyes looked rather wild.

'I've come to borrow a cigarette from you, Jeeves. I appear to have lost my cigarette-case. Seen it anywhere?'

'I am sorry to hear that, sir. It is not in the car, sir.'

'No? Must have dropped it somewhere, then.' I lit his cigarette, which he smoked quickly and a little desperately.

'Jolly creatures, small girls, Jeeves,' he said, after a while.

'Extremely, sir.'

'Of course, I can imagine some fellows finding them a bit exhausting – er – in large numbers.'

'I must confess, sir, that I used to feel that myself. In my younger days, sir, I was a servant at a school for young ladies.'

'No, really? I never knew that before. I say, Jeeves, did the – er – dear little things *giggle* much in your day?'

'Almost all the time, sir.'

'Makes a fellow feel rather silly, doesn't it? Perhaps they used to stare at you from time to time, too, did they?'

'Yes, sir. The young ladies played a regular game every time a gentleman visitor arrived at the school. They used to stare fixedly at him and giggle, and there was a small prize for the one who made his face redden first.'

'Oh, no, I say, Jeeves, not really? I'd no idea small girls were such devils.'

'Much worse than small boys, sir.'

Mr Wooster passed a hand over his forehead. 'Well, we're going to have tea in a few minutes, Jeeves. I expect I'll feel better after tea.'

'We will hope so, sir.' But I was not confident of this.

After I had had my tea in the kitchen with the cook and the other servants, I returned to the garage. In a few moments Mr Wooster appeared, looking deeply worried.

'Jeeves! Start the car! I'm leaving! Don't look at me like a fish, Jeeves! Just start the car! The situation's desperate. The Tomlinson woman has just told me I've got to stand up in front of the whole dashed school and give a talk! Hurry up, Jeeves, dash it! A little speed, a little speed!'

'Impossible, I fear, sir. The car is not working.'

'Not working!' Mr Wooster's mouth fell open, as he stared at me in horror. I am fond of Mr Wooster, and I confess I came near to melting as I looked at his pale, anxious face.

'Do you think,' he said, with a sudden, hopeful light in his eyes, 'I could escape across the fields on foot, Jeeves?'

'Too late, I fear, sir.' Behind him I could see the figure of Miss Tomlinson moving purposefully towards us.

'Ah, there you are, Mr Wooster.'

He smiled weakly. 'Yes – er – here I am!'

'We are all waiting for you in the large schoolroom.'

'But, I say, I don't know at all what to talk about.'

'Oh, anything, Mr Wooster. Be bright and amusing. But at the same time, do not forget to give my girls a serious message, something brave and helpful and encouraging, something they can remember in future years. But of course you know the sort of thing, Mr Wooster. Come. The young people are waiting.'

As I have said, resource is a necessary quality for a gentleman's personal gentleman. In this case, I had to be resourceful in order to witness Mr Wooster's talk to the young ladies. Fortunately, it was a fine day and the schoolroom windows were wide open, so I was able to stand outside, and see and hear everything that happened inside. It was an experience which I would be sorry to have missed.

Mr Wooster was standing unhappily at one end of a large hall. Two or three hundred girls were sitting in front of him, all staring fixedly at him. He was introduced by Miss Tomlinson.

'Girls, I hope you have all heard of Mr Bertram Wooster. He has very kindly agreed to say a few words to you before he leaves the school. Now, please.'

She lifted her hand, and at this signal, two things happened. Mr Wooster started speaking, and the girls began to sing a song of greeting. This seemed to alarm Mr Wooster, who threw up his arm and stepped quickly backwards. When the song came to an end, and there was silence again, he took an unsteady step forward, and said, 'Well, you know – er – ladies—' Silvery laughter rang out from the front row.

'Girls!' said Miss Tomlinson. She spoke in a low, soft voice, but the effect was immediate. Perfect stillness fell upon the room.

By now I imagine that Miss Tomlinson had realized how limited Mr Wooster's speaking ability was. 'Perhaps,' she said, 'as it is getting late, Mr Wooster will just give you some little word of advice, and then we will sing the school song, and start our evening lessons. Mr Wooster?'

'Oh, well – yes – well—' It was painful to see Mr Wooster's brain attempting to work. 'Well, I'll tell you something not many people know. My old Uncle Henry told me this when I first came to London. "Never forget, my boy," he said, "that you can see the clock in Fleet Street from Romano's restaurant in the Strand." Most people don't believe it's possible, you see,

41

so it's worth knowing, because you can make a lot of money by betting on it with fellows who haven't found out yet—'

'Mr Wooster,' said Miss Tomlinson, in a cold, hard voice, 'perhaps it would be better if you told my girls some little story. What you say is no doubt extremely interesting, but—'

'Oh, ah, yes,' said Mr Wooster. 'Story? Story? I wonder if you've heard the one about the businessman and the actress?'

'We will now sing the school song,' said Miss Tomlinson icily, rising to her feet.

It was painful to see Mr Wooster's brain attempting to work.

It seemed probable to me that Mr Wooster would soon need the car, so I walked back to the garage. I did not have long to wait. In a very few moments he appeared, pale and trembling. I can read his face like a book, and there was strong feeling in his expression.

'Jeeves,' he said, 'is that dashed car mended yet?'

'Just this moment, sir. I have been working on it.'

'Then let's go, by Jove!'

'But I understood that you were going to speak to the young ladies, sir.'

'Oh, I've done that! Yes, I've done that.'

'It was a success, I hope, sir?'

'Oh, yes. Oh, yes. Most extraordinarily successful. But – er – I think it's time to leave. Mustn't stay too long, you know.'

I had climbed into the car and was about to start the engine, when I heard a voice. As soon as he heard it, Mr Wooster jumped down on to the floor of the car and covered himself with a coat. I could just see an anxious eye looking wildly up at me.

'Have you seen Mr Wooster, my man?' asked Miss Tomlinson. She seemed to have lost her usual calmness.

'No, madam. Is anything wrong, madam?'

'Yes, there is!' she replied angrily. 'We have just found several of the girls smoking cigarettes in the garden. When questioned, they said Mr Wooster had given them the horrible things.' She turned away. 'Perhaps he's in the house, then. I shall look for him there. I think the man is mad!'

It must have been about a minute later that Mr Wooster's head appeared from under the coat.

'Jeeves!'

'Sir?'

'Hurry up! Start the engine! Start driving and *don't stop*!'

'It would perhaps be safest to drive carefully until we are out of the school grounds, sir. I might run down one of the young ladies, sir.'

'Well, what's wrong with that?' demanded Mr Wooster, with extraordinary bitterness.

'Or even Miss Tomlinson, sir.'

'Don't speak of it!' said Mr Wooster, with a sigh. 'It's a delicious thought!'

'Jeeves,' said Mr Wooster, when I brought him his whisky one night about a week later, 'this is dashed jolly.'

'Sir?'

'Jolly. Cosy and pleasant, you know. I mean, here you come with the good old drinks, always on time, putting them on the table and staggering off, and the next night the same old thing, and the next night – I mean, it gives you a sort of safe, restful feeling.'

'Yes, sir. Oh, by the way, sir, have you succeeded in finding a suitable house yet, sir?'

'House? What do you mean, house?'

'I understood, sir, that you were intending to give up the flat and take a house large enough for your sister, Mrs Scholfield, and her three young ladies to live with you.'

Mr Wooster went quite pale and shook his head firmly.

'That's off, Jeeves,' he said.

'Very good, sir,' I replied.

Looking After the Pumpkin

The morning sunshine fell gently on Blandings Castle, showing its ancient walls, its parks, and its gardens in a cheerful light. It fell on smooth green grass, on great trees and bright flower-beds. It fell on the large trouser-covered bottom of Angus McAllister, Scottish head-gardener to the ninth Earl of Emsworth, as he bent to remove an insect from a flower. It fell on the white trousers of the Hon. Freddie Threepwood, Lord Emsworth's younger son, hurrying across a nearby field. It also fell on Lord Emsworth himself, and on Beach, his butler. They were standing at the top of the castle tower, Lord Emsworth with his eye to a large telescope, Beach holding his lordship's hat.

'Beach,' said Lord Emsworth. 'This dashed thing doesn't work. I can't see through it at all. It's all black.'

'Perhaps if I removed the cover at the end of the telescope, my lord . . .'

'Eh? Cover? Is there a cover? Well, take it off, Beach.'

'Very good, my lord.'

'Ah.' Lord Emsworth sounded happier. 'Yes, that's better. That's very good. Beach, I can see a cow.'

'Indeed, my lord?'

'Down in the field. Remarkable. Could be only two metres away. All right, Beach. Shan't want you any longer.'

'Your hat, my lord?'

'Put it on my head.'

'Very good, my lord.' The butler did so, and departed. Lord Emsworth went on staring through the telescope.

The ninth Earl of Emsworth was a likeable, if forgetful, old gentleman. Although the main interest of his life was his garden, he had a fondness for new toys. He had seen the telescope advertised in a magazine, and ordered it from London. It had been delivered the previous day, and now the moment had come to try it out.

Soon he began to lose interest in the cow. It was a fine cow, compared with other cows, but, like so many cows, it provided no excitement for the audience. It just ate the grass and stared vacantly at nothing. Lord Emsworth was just going to find something a little more sensational to look at, when the Hon. Freddie came into sight. White and shining, he walked through the field with a confident step and a bright smile.

Lord Emsworth frowned suddenly. He usually frowned when he saw Freddie, because, with the passing of the years, that young man had become more and more of a problem to an anxious father. If he was allowed to live in London, he spent far too much money, and got into trouble, but if he was kept in the more innocent surroundings of Blandings Castle, he just became depressed and miserable. Lord Emsworth did not enjoy having a moody young man in his home.

However, at the moment Freddie's appearance was so unusually and mysteriously cheerful that Lord Emsworth continued to watch him through the telescope. A small voice inside the earl's head seemed to whisper, 'That young man is planning to do something he shouldn't.'

And the small voice was absolutely correct. His lordship just had time to wish, as he usually did when he saw his son, that Freddie were completely different in manners and appearance, and the son of somebody else living a considerable distance away, when a girl came running out of a wood at the end of the field. Freddie, after a cautious look over his shoulder, took her warmly in his arms and kissed her.

Lord Emsworth had seen enough. He staggered away from the telescope, a broken man. One of his favourite dreams was of some nice, well-behaved girl, belonging to a good family and with some money of her own, who would come along one day and marry Freddie, but the small voice in his head told him that this was not the girl he had dreamed of. No, there was only one explanation. Even here, in the simple quietness of Blandings, far from the great, busy capital, where that kind of thing was so easily available, Freddie had managed to find an unsuitable girl to fall in love with.

Angrily, Lord Emsworth hurried down the stairs, and out into the garden. Here he walked up and down, like an old tiger waiting for feeding-time, until Freddie appeared, whistling cheerfully, and with a sheep-like smile on his face.

'Frederick!' shouted his lordship.

Freddie stopped at once. Lost in his dreams, he had not noticed his father. But his mood was so sunny that even this meeting could not depress him. 'Hullo, father!' he cried happily. He searched for something pleasant to talk about – always a matter of some difficulty on these occasions. 'Lovely day, don't you think?'

His lordship refused to discuss the weather. There were other, more important things to talk about. 'Frederick,' he demanded, frowning deeply, 'who was that girl?'

The Hon. Freddie gave a little jump. 'Girl?' he asked, his voice trembling. 'Girl? Girl, father?'

'That girl I saw you kissing ten minutes ago, in the field.'

'Oh!' said the Hon. Freddie. He paused. 'Oh, ah!' He paused again. 'I've been meaning to tell you about that, father.'

'You have, have you?'

'All perfectly correct, you know. Oh, yes, indeed! Nothing, you know, not quite right, or anything like that. She's my fiancée.'

A sharp cry came from Lord Emsworth. 'Who is she? Who is this woman?'

'Her name's Aggie Donaldson. She's – er – American.'

'Who is she?'

'She's awfully intelligent, you know. You'll love her.'

'Who is she?'

'And she's terribly good at jazz on the piano.'

'Who', demanded Lord Emsworth for the fifth time, 'is she? And where did you meet her?'

Freddie knew that he could no longer keep back the information. He also knew that his father would not greet the news with cries of delight. 'Well, as a matter of fact, father, she's a sort of cousin of Angus McAllister's. She's come over to England for a visit, don't you know, and is staying with the old boy. That's how I happened to meet her.'

Lord Emsworth's eyes opened wide, and a strange, wordless sound came from his mouth. His worst fears for his son's future had never included marriage to a sort of cousin of his head-gardener. 'Oh!' he said. 'Oh, indeed?'

'That's it, father.'

Lord Emsworth threw his arms up hopelessly, and started running along the path through the gardens. He soon found the person he was looking for.

The head-gardener turned at the sound of his footsteps. He

was a well-built man of medium height, with bushy eyebrows and a thick red beard, which gave him a fierce and unbending expression. His face showed honesty, and also intelligence, but it was a bit short of sweetness and light.

'McAllister,' said his lordship urgently, 'that girl. You must send her away.'

'Girrrl?' asked McAllister, looking puzzled.

'That girl who is staying with you. She must go!'

'Go where?'

Lord Emsworth was not in the mood to worry about details. 'Anywhere. You must send her away immediately.'

'I cannae,' said McAllister simply. 'She's paying me twa pounds a week for her food.'

Lord Emsworth jumped some thirty centimetres into the air. He completely forgot that he was normally a reasonable man, well aware that even earls must think twice before ordering their employees about. 'Listen, McAllister! Listen to me! Either you send that girl away today or you can go yourself! I mean it!'

A strange expression came over McAllister's face. It was the look of a Scot who has not forgotten his country's past battles against the English. He made Scottish noises at the back of his throat.

'Your lorrrdship will accept my notice,' he said firmly.

'I'll pay you a month's wages instead of notice and you will leave this afternoon,' replied Lord Emsworth heatedly.

'Mmhm!' said Mr McAllister.

As he left the battlefield, Lord Emsworth felt extremely pleased with himself. But that night, as he sat smoking his after-dinner cigarette, reason returned to its usual seat, and a cold hand seemed suddenly placed on his heart.

*Now that Angus McAllister had gone,
who would look after the pumpkin?*

Now that Angus McAllister had gone, who would look after
the pumpkin?

The importance of this pumpkin in the Earl of Emsworth's
life needs, perhaps, a word of explanation. For hundreds of
years the ancient family of Emsworths had done great and good
things for their country. They had been soldiers, officers,
politicians, and leaders of the people. But they had not, in Lord
Emsworth's opinion, succeeded in everything, because the fact
remained that no Earl of Emsworth had ever won a first prize
for a pumpkin at the Shrewsbury Agricultural Show. For roses,
yes. For carrots, true. For potatoes, all right. But not for
pumpkins, and Lord Emsworth felt it deeply.

For many years he had been working hard to win this prize
for the Emsworths, and this year, at last, he had his best chance
of winning. As he looked lovingly at his pumpkin's golden
roundness, he felt sure that even Sir Gregory Parsloe-Parsloe

of Matchingham Hall, his neighbour and the pumpkin prizewinner for the last three years, could never produce anything to challenge this wonderful vegetable.

But now he feared that, by sacking his head-gardener, he might lose the prize, because Angus McAllister was the pumpkin's official trainer. He understood it, and even seemed to love it, in his silent Scottish way. Could the pumpkin survive without him? Lord Emsworth tried to tell himself that McAllister was not the only man in the world who understood pumpkins, and that he had complete confidence in Robert Barker, the new head-gardener now responsible for looking after the Blandings hope. However, it soon became clear that Robert Barker did not have McAllister's magic touch, and would not be able to produce a winner. Within a week Lord Emsworth began to miss Angus McAllister.

It seemed to him that the pumpkin was missing Angus too. He had a terrible feeling it was actually getting smaller, every day. And so, only ten days after McAllister's departure, he knew what he had to do.

Fortunately, Beach had McAllister's address in London, and Lord Emsworth sent the following telegram:

McALLISTER 11 BUXTON CRESCENT LONDON
RETURN IMMEDIATELY — EMSWORTH

The reply came speedily back:

LORD EMSWORTH BLANDINGS CASTLE SHROPSHIRE
I WILL NOT — McALLISTER

Lord Emsworth, whose brain could only hold one thought at a time, had not considered the possibility of McAllister refusing to return. It took him the whole day to get used to this new problem, but he managed to solve it at last. Robert Barker could remain in charge for another day or so. Meanwhile he himself would go to London to find a real head-gardener, the finest head-gardener that money could buy.

It was the opinion of Dr Johnson, the famous eighteenth-century writer, that London offers everything that anyone could need. He once said that a man who is tired of London is tired of life. Lord Emsworth would have disagreed hotly with Dr Johnson. He hated London, its crowds, its smells, its noises, its buses, its taxis, and its hard pavements. And in addition to all its other faults, the miserable town did not seem able to provide a single good head-gardener. For three whole days, he went from agency to agency, but not one of the men he interviewed came anywhere near meeting his needs. It was a hard thing to say of any man, but he doubted whether even the best of them was as good as Robert Barker.

It was, therefore, in a black and bitter mood that his lordship stood on the steps of his club, where he had just had a light lunch. He was wondering how to spend his afternoon. Tomorrow, more interviews with gardeners were planned, but meanwhile, what could a man of reasonable tastes do with his time in this hopeless town? And then he remembered Kensington Gardens, famous all over the country for its flowers. He could go there, and give his soul a chance to breathe.

He was about to call a taxi, when suddenly he saw a young man come out of the hotel opposite and walk towards the club. As he came closer, Lord Emsworth seemed to recognize him. He stared for a long moment before he could believe his eyes, then with a wordless cry ran down the steps just as the young man started to climb them.

'Oh, hullo, father!' cried the Hon. Freddie, clearly surprised.

'What – what are you doing here?' demanded Lord Emsworth angrily. London was forbidden ground to Freddie. His adventures there still lived on in the mind of a father who had had to pay the bills.

The young man was looking rather uncomfortable. 'The fact is, father—'

'You know you are forbidden to come to London. And why anybody but a complete fool would want to come to London when he could be at Blandings—'

'I know, father, but the fact is – I wanted to see you.'

This was not quite true. The last thing in the world that the Hon. Freddie wanted to see was his parent. He had only come to his father's club to leave a carefully written note for him. This unexpected meeting had upset his plans.

'To see me?' said Lord Emsworth. 'Why?'

'Got – er – something to tell you. Dashed important. I say, father, can you take a bit of a shock?'

A terrible thought rushed into Lord Emsworth's mind. Freddie's mysterious arrival in London – his strange manner – could it mean—? He took hold of the young man's arm feverishly. 'Frederick! Speak! Tell me! Have the cats got at it?'

Freddie stared. 'Cats? Why? Where? Which cats?'

'Frederick! Is anything wrong with the pumpkin?'

Unfortunately, in this rushed and insensitive world, there are a few people here and there whose souls are not moved by pumpkins. Freddie was one of these; his father's anxious question just made him giggle and shake his head.

'Then what do you mean,' thundered Lord Emsworth, 'by

frightening me – frightening me nearly to death, by Jove! – with your nonsense about giving me shocks?'

The Hon. Freddie produced a note from his pocket. 'Look here, father,' he said shakily, 'I think the best thing will be for you to read this. It's – well – you just read it. Goodbye, father. Got to rush.' And, pushing the note into his father's hand, the Hon. Freddie turned and disappeared.

Lord Emsworth read the note. It was short, but full of interest.

Dear father,

Awfully sorry and all that, but couldn't wait any longer. I've come up to London in your car, and Aggie and I got married this morning. Aggie's father has come over from America, and wants to see you. You'll like him. Well, goodbye for now.

Your loving son, Freddie

P.S. You won't mind if I keep the car for the moment, will you? It may be useful for our wedding trip.

It is not too much to say Lord Emsworth was shaken to the centre of his being. He was deeply depressed at the thought of supporting, for the rest of his life, a younger son, a younger son's wife, and possibly younger grandchildren.

Suddenly, an urgent need for flowers and green trees came over him. He signalled wildly to a passing taxi. 'Kensington Gardens,' he said, and, getting in, sat down with a sigh of relief.

Something like peace began to enter his lordship's soul as he entered the cool shade of the park. 'Ah!' he breathed delightedly, as he stopped in front of a whole bed of roses. A beautiful flower-bed has an effect like a drug on men who love their gardens, and Lord Emsworth had already completely forgotten where he was. He seemed to be back in his lovely garden at Blandings. He went closer, and bent to pick first one rose, then a second, then a third.

'Hi!!!' shouted a park-keeper. 'Hi there! Stop that!'

Lord Emsworth looked up, alarmed, and realized where he was. 'Oh dear, I'm so sorry,' he said.

The park-keeper spoke loudly and rapidly. It was clear that he considered Lord Emsworth the blackest type of criminal. People began to gather round, and soon there was quite an interested crowd. And then a large, solid policeman arrived. He asked for the criminal's name and address.

Lord Emsworth was feeling weak and confused. 'I – why, my dear fellow – I mean, officer – I am the Earl of Emsworth.'

The crowd looked at the old man, who was wearing a badly fitting suit and a hat anyone ought to be ashamed of, and laughed. They laughed even more loudly when Lord Emsworth was unable to find any papers to prove who he was. Just then two more men joined the crowd – one a tall, handsome gentleman with glasses, the other a shorter man with a thick red beard. Lord Emsworth recognized the beard at once.

'McAllister!' he cried. 'McAllister, my dear chap, do please tell the officer who I am.'

A lesser man would have taken his revenge here, but not Angus McAllister. He stepped forward. 'That's Lorrrd Emsworrrth,' he said firmly.

The policeman looked at the Scot's honest face and accepted his word. Being unwilling to arrest a lord, he ordered the crowd to move along. Soon Lord Emsworth was left alone with McAllister and the tall gentleman with glasses, who now spoke to the earl.

'Pleased to meet you at last,' he said. 'My name is Donaldson.

I think we should talk.' He fixed Lord Emsworth with a confident, business-like look.

Lord Emsworth, suddenly recognizing the name, stared back at him angrily, but there was something in the other's calm grey eyes that made him hesitate.

'How do you do?' he said weakly.

'*McAllister, do please tell the officer who I am.*'

'Now listen, Lord Emsworth. You've heard by now that your boy and my girl have got married? Personally, I'm delighted. That boy is a fine young fellow.'

Lord Emsworth did not believe what he had just heard. 'You are speaking of my son Frederick?' he said.

'Of your son Frederick. Perhaps you're a little angry with him just now, but you must forgive him. He needs your support.'

'I suppose so. Can't let the boy die of hunger.'

'Don't you worry about that. I'll take care of that side of things. I'm not a rich man—'

'Oh!' said Lord Emsworth sadly. The man's appearance and manner had begun to raise his hopes.

'I doubt,' continued Mr Donaldson, who was a man who believed in openness in these matters, 'if I have as much as ten million dollars in the world.'

'Ten million? Did you say you had ten million dollars?'

'Between nine and ten million, no more. Life has been tough for us in America lately. But now the American dog is beginning to eat more biscuits. That's my business, you see. I am Donaldson's Dog Biscuits.'

'Really? Indeed? Well, well!' said Lord Emsworth.

'Yes, and I am in a position to offer Freddie a good job in my company. I want to send him over to New York to start learning the business. Can I tell him, Lord Emsworth, that he has his father's support in this?'

'Yes, yes, yes!' said Lord Emsworth warmly. Suddenly his heart was full of love for Mr Donaldson. He himself had been trying to get rid of Freddie for twenty-six years, and now this god-like man had done it in less than a week.

'My daughter and he sail to New York on Wednesday.'

'Excellent!'

'May I give them a forgiving, friendly message from you?'

'Certainly, certainly, certainly. Inform Frederick that he has my best wishes.'

'I will.'

'Mention that I hope he will work hard and make a name for himself.'

'Exactly.'

'And,' finished Lord Emsworth, speaking with a well-judged fatherly seriousness, 'tell him – er – not to hurry home.'

He shook Mr Donaldson's hand with feelings too deep to express. Then he rushed over to where Angus McAllister stood looking thoughtfully at the rose-bed.

'McAllister!'

The head-gardener looked at his former employer with cold eyes. Lord Emsworth forced himself to speak.

'McAllister – I wish – I wonder – whether you have accepted another post yet?'

'I am considering twa.'

'Come back to me!' begged his lordship, his voice breaking. 'Robert Barker is worse than useless!'

McAllister stared woodenly at the roses. 'I will—' he began at last, very slowly.

'You will?' cried Lord Emsworth delightedly. 'Excellent!'

'I didn't say I would,' said McAllister stiffly. 'I was going to say "I will consider it".'

Lord Emsworth put a trembling hand on his shoulder. 'McAllister, I will raise your salary. Dash it, I'll pay you twice as much!'

McAllister's eyebrows rose, and his beard moved from side to side.

'McAllister . . . Angus . . .' said Lord Emsworth in a low voice. 'Come back! The pumpkin needs you.'

In an age of rush and hurry like today's, it is possible that here and there among the readers of this story there may be one or two who, for various reasons, found themselves unable to attend the most recent Agricultural Show at Shrewsbury. For these people a few words must be added.

Sir Gregory Parsloe-Parsloe of Matchingham Hall was there, of course, but looking noticeably less happy than in previous years. However, he was a gentleman and a sportsman. In the tent where the vegetables were on show, he bravely offered his hand to Lord Emsworth.

'Congratulate you, Emsworth,' he said, with some difficulty.

Lord Emsworth looked up, surprised. He had been deep in his thoughts. 'Eh? Oh, thank you very much, my dear fellow. Er – can't both win, can we?'

Sir Gregory thought about it for a moment. 'No,' he said. 'See what you mean. Can't both win. That's right.'

He walked away, hiding the pain in his manly heart. And Lord Emsworth, with Angus McAllister at his side, turned once more to look lovingly at what lay in one of the largest boxes ever seen in Shrewsbury. A card was attached to the box. It said:

PUMPKINS – FIRST PRIZE

Lord Emsworth and the Girl Friend

The day was so warm, so magically sunny, that anyone who knew how much Clarence, ninth Earl of Emsworth, loved fine weather, would have imagined him going around Blandings Castle on this summer morning with a happy smile and a light heart. Instead of this, he was sitting at the breakfast table, staring bitterly at his boiled egg. It was the first Monday in August, a public holiday, and on this day Blandings Castle became, in his lordship's opinion, hell on earth.

This was the day when the castle was opened to the public, when a great wave of villagers and their screaming children disturbed the peace of Lord Emsworth's home, when tents and tables and chairs appeared all over his beautiful grounds, and the noise of loud music, cries and shouts filled the normally quiet air. On this day he was not allowed to walk around the gardens in his old clothes. His sister, Lady Constance, always forced him to wear a stiff collar and top hat, and expected him to talk cheerfully to people. Worst of all, after tea had been served in the main tent, she made him give a speech. To a man with a day like that ahead of him, fine weather was no help at all.

'What a lovely morning!' said Lady Constance brightly. 'I hope you have got your speech ready, Clarence. Make sure you learn it by heart this time, and don't hesitate over it, as you did last year.'

Lord Emsworth pushed his uneaten egg away. He no longer felt hungry.

'And don't forget to go to the village today. Remember, you are judging the villagers' gardens, to find the best-kept one.'

'All right, all right, all right,' said his lordship crossly. 'I haven't forgotten.'

'I will come to the village too. There are a number of children from London staying there for a few days, and I must warn them to behave properly when they come to the Open Day this afternoon. McAllister says he found one of them in the castle gardens the other day, picking the flowers.'

Lord Emsworth was feeling so sorry for himself that he did not even appear shocked by this news. Miserably he drank his coffee, wishing it were poisoned.

'By the way, McAllister was speaking to me again about that gravel path. He seems very enthusiastic about the idea.'

'Gravel path!' cried Lord Emsworth angrily. 'Dash it all, I'm not having that lovely grassy path turned into gravel! Why not make it a road, with a petrol station and a fish and chip shop? That's what the man would really like!'

Lord Emsworth spoke with extreme bitterness, because he hated even having to think about Angus McAllister's plan. For years, the head-gardener at Blandings, a red-bearded, hard-faced Scot, had wanted to build a gravel path between the two lines of ancient trees leading up to the castle. Lord Emsworth felt strongly that the present grassy path, which his family had used for centuries, was what Mother Nature had intended, and should be kept as it was.

'Well, I think it is a very good idea,' said his sister. 'I could walk there in bad weather then, without getting my feet wet on the grass.'

Lord Emsworth got up. He had had enough of this. He left the table, the room, and the house, and, reaching the path in question, was unpleasantly surprised to find Angus McAllister standing on it. The head-gardener was looking fixedly down at the ground. His feelings were clear; he was totally opposed to grass, and he wanted gravel. Lord Emsworth wondered why God, if forced to make head-gardeners, had found it necessary to make them so Scottish. In the case of McAllister, why make him a human being at all? He would have been a really excellent mule. Lord Emsworth felt he might have liked Angus McAllister if he had been a mule.

'Morning, McAllister,' said Lord Emsworth coldly.

'Good morrrning, your lorrrdship.' There was a pause. 'About the grrravel path, your lorrrdship . . .' Another pause.

Filled with anger, Lord Emsworth was about to tell McAllister exactly what he thought about the gravel path, when suddenly he stopped. He had just realized how much he needed McAllister. This man was a head-gardener in a thousand, and Lord Emsworth could not manage without him. Once before, in that business with the pumpkin, Angus had given notice, and Lord Emsworth had had to beg him to return to Blandings. He could not now give the man orders and expect him to obey them. He was helpless.

'I'll – er – I'll consider it, McAllister.'

'Mmhm,' said McAllister.

It did not sound to Lord Emsworth like an acceptance of defeat.

Lord Emsworth usually looked forward to judging the villagers' gardens, but today he was feeling low. It is always unpleasant for a proud man to realize that he is no longer captain of his soul, and that he is just like a bit of dirt under the boot of his Scottish head-gardener. Deep in these depressing thoughts, he did not concentrate fully on the judging until he came to the last house on his list.

'Not a bad little garden at all,' he said to himself, as he opened the gate and walked in. He bent to smell some colourful wallflowers, and just then he was violently attacked by a small but very fierce dog. Lord Emsworth forgot his interest in the wallflowers, wishing only to save his ankles from harm. He was not at his best with strange dogs, and was still jumping about ineffectively, saying, 'Go away, sir!' rather desperately, when the door of the house opened and a girl came out.

'Stop that!' cried the girl. At the first sound of her voice, the dog turned and ran obediently to her, throwing itself on its back with all four legs in the air. This sight reminded the earl of his own behaviour when in the presence of Angus McAllister.

He looked with interest at his rescuer. She was a small girl, only twelve or thirteen, but capable-looking and motherly. She was the type of girl you sometimes see in London back streets, in charge of several younger brothers and sisters. Her face was washed, and her hair was brushed, and she was obviously wearing her best dress.

'Er – thank you,' said Lord Emsworth.

'Thank you, sir,' said the girl. It was not clear what she was thanking him for, but later, after further conversations, Lord Emsworth discovered that his new friend had a habit of thanking everyone for everything.

He searched for something to talk about. He was not used to making conversation with young women.

'Do you – er – live here?'

'No, sir. I ain't from the village, I'm from London, sir. I'm just staying here.'

'Ah? London? The weather must be warm there at the moment.' Then he remembered what people used to ask when he was younger. 'Been to many dances this season?'

'No, sir.'

'Everybody's at their country homes by now, I suppose. What's your name?'

'Gladys, sir. Thank you, sir. And this is my brother Ern.'

A small boy had come out of the house. To the earl's surprise, he was carrying an armful of beautiful flowers.

'How do you do?' said Lord Emsworth politely. 'What pretty flowers.'

'Lovely, ain't they?' said Gladys happily. 'I picked them for Ern up at the castle, and the old man who owns the place saw me and chased me. But I threw a stone at him and hit his leg and so I escaped.'

Lord Emsworth was so full of admiration that he didn't bother to explain that Blandings Castle and its gardens belonged to him and not to Angus McAllister. This super-woman not only controlled aggressive dogs with a word, she also threw stones at McAllister – something the earl had never been brave enough to do – and what was more, hit him on the leg. Was this what the Modern Girl was like? He could not imagine a more perfect example of Woman.

'We're going to the Open Day in the park this afternoon,' said Gladys.

For the first time Lord Emsworth began to think about that awful social event with something like interest. 'I hope to see you there,' he said warmly. 'You will recognize me? I shall be wearing' – he swallowed – 'a top hat. Well, goodbye for now.'

'Goodbye, sir. Thank you, sir.'

Lord Emsworth walked out of the garden, and, turning into the little street, met Lady Constance.

'Oh, there you are, Clarence. I hope you have finished judging the gardens. I am just going to have a word with the little girl in that house. I want to warn her to behave herself this afternoon. I have spoken to the others.'

Lord Emsworth straightened his shoulders and looked commandingly at his sister. 'Well, be careful what you say, Constance. I greatly admire the young lady about whom you

'Oh, there you are, Clarence,' said Lady Constance.

are speaking. She has behaved on two recent occasions with bravery and resource, and I won't have her upset. Understand that!'

From under the shadow of his top hat, Lord Emsworth miserably watched the villagers enjoying themselves. He simply could not understand why adults who, for three hundred and sixty-four days in the year, were normal, polite, and reasonable, should on the first Monday in August go completely mad, and run around shouting, drinking out of bottles, singing songs and playing childish games. The worst of it was that they were doing it in his private park. How would they like it, he thought bitterly, if he went and ran around shouting in their little gardens?

And it was always so hellishly hot. July could end with a fall of snow, but as soon as the first Monday in August arrived and he had to put on a stiff collar, out came the sun, making him feel extremely uncomfortable. Of course, there were advantages and disadvantages to the heat. The hotter the day, the more quickly his collar lost its horrible stiffness. At the moment it felt like a wet bandage round his neck, so, although he was suffering, he realized things could be worse.

A masterful figure appeared at his side. 'Clarence!'

Lord Emsworth now felt so depressed that not even the arrival of his sister Constance could add noticeably to his discomfort.

'Clarence, you look perfectly terrible.'

'I know I do. Who wouldn't, in a stiff collar and top hat? Why do you always insist on . . .'

'Please don't be childish, Clarence. For once in your life you must dress like an English gentleman, not a homeless beggar.

And stiff collars are what I came to speak to you about. Look at yours! Go in and change it at once.'

'But, my dear Constance . . .'

'At once, Clarence. I simply cannot understand a man with so little interest in his appearance. But all your life you have been like that. I remember when we were children . . .'

Lord Emsworth's past was not so innocent that he felt like staying to hear his sister discuss it. She had an excellent memory. 'Oh, all right, all right, all right,' he said. 'I'll change it.'

'Well, hurry. They are just starting tea.'

Lord Emsworth trembled. 'Have I got to go into the tea-tent?'

'Of course you have. Don't be so silly. I do wish you would remember your position. As lord of Blandings Castle . . .'

A bitter, hollow laugh from the poor, weak fellow described as 'lord' drowned the rest of her words.

It always seemed to Lord Emsworth that the Open Day Hell at Blandings Castle reached the height of awfulness when tea was served in the large tent, and then again soon afterwards, when the moment came for him to make his speech. After that, the horror passed slowly away until the following August.

This year, the temperature in the tea-tent was the highest in living memory, and Lord Emsworth was pleased to find that his second collar almost immediately began to lose its iron stiffness. That, however, was the only moment of happiness he was to have. It took his experienced eye only a few seconds to realize that the present tea-party was going to be far worse than any previous ones.

The village children, although noisy, were generally quite easy to control. What was giving the tea-tent the air of an aggressive political meeting was the unfortunate presence of the children from London. A London child, in his constant battles with parents, teachers, and other adults, speedily loses any shyness or modesty he once had, and when he notices something amusing, is quick to remark on it. Lord Emsworth did not normally think fast, but on this occasion he felt it would be sensible to take off his top hat before his little guests noticed it.

This was, however, not necessary. As he raised his hand, a small cake, whistling through the air, took it off for him.

Lord Emsworth had had enough. Even Constance, that unreasonable woman, could not possibly expect him to stay and smile cheerfully in a situation where law and order had completely broken down. He cautiously made his way to the exit, and departed.

Outside the tent, the world was quieter, but not quiet enough. Lord Emsworth hurried to the one place in the whole park where he felt sure he would be alone. This was a small shed, once used for cows. But as he began to enjoy the peace and the coolness, he heard a noise from one of the dark corners, and realized, with some annoyance, that someone had got there before him.

'Who's that?' he asked angrily.

'Me, sir. Thank you, sir.'

There was only one person Lord Emsworth knew who was capable of thanking someone for an angry question. His anger died away at once.

'By Jove! What are you doing in a cowshed?'

'Please, sir, the lady put me here, for stealing things, sir. Two jam sandwiches, two apples and two slices of cake.' Gladys had come out of her dark corner, and Lord Emsworth could see tears on her face. No Emsworth had ever been able to watch a woman crying. The ninth earl was visibly moved.

'Did you eat them?'

'No, sir, they weren't for me, they were for Ern.'

Lord Emsworth didn't think much of these modern young men, if they made their women do all the dirty work. 'But why couldn't Ern – er – steal them for himself?'

'Ern wasn't allowed to come to the Open Day, sir.'

'What! Not allowed? Who said he wasn't allowed?'

'The lady who came in just after you this morning, sir.'

'Ah!' thought Lord Emsworth, 'Constance! Changing my guest list just like that! One of these days she'll go too far!'

'Ern was playing, sir. He pretended to be a dog and bit her on the leg, sir. She was cross and said he couldn't come. So I planned to bring him back something nice, to cheer him up.'

Lord Emsworth breathed heavily. What a family! The sister threw stones at McAllister, the brother bit Constance on the leg . . . Such bravery, such fearlessness . . . It showed there was still something to admire in the modern world.

'I thought it'd be all right, sir, if I didn't have nothing myself. Thank you, sir.'

'Nothing? Do you mean to tell me you haven't had tea?'

'No, sir. I thought if I didn't have nothing, then it would be all right for Ern to have what I would have had if I had had.'

His lordship's head, never strong, swam a little. Then he understood. 'By Jove! I never heard anything so terrible in my life! Come with me immediately.'

'The lady said I had to stay here, sir.'

'Oh, bother the lady!'

'Yes, sir. Thank you, sir.'

Five minutes later, Beach, the butler, was awoken from his afternoon sleep by the unexpected ringing of a bell. When he went to answer it, he found his employer in the sitting-room, with a rather surprising young person. Beach, having excellent self-control, kept his face expressionless.

'Oh, Beach, this young lady would like some tea.'

'Very good, your lordship.'

'Cake, you know. And apples, and jam sandwiches, and that sort of thing. And she has a brother, Beach.'

'Indeed, your lordship.'

'She will want to take some food away for him.' Lord Emsworth turned to his guest. 'Ernest would like a little chicken perhaps? Some cold meat? Some cheese?'

'Oh, yes, sir. Thank you, sir.'

'And put in a bottle of the wine that was delivered last week, Beach. It's nothing special,' he explained to his guest, 'but quite drinkable. I would like your brother's opinion of it. Put it all together in a basket, Beach, and leave it on the table in the hall. We will pick it up as we go out.'

A welcome coolness was in the air by the time Lord Emsworth and his guest came out of the great door of the castle. Gladys, holding the basket and the earl's hand, sighed happily. She had eaten a large tea. Life seemed to have nothing more to offer. But Lord Emsworth thought differently.

'Now, is there anything else you can think of that Ernest would like?' he asked. 'Do not hesitate to mention it.'

A hopeful look came into Gladys's eyes. 'Could he have some flarze?'

'Certainly, certainly, certainly. Just what I was going to

suggest myself – er – what *is* flarze?'

Fortunately Beach, who was good at languages, was able to help. 'I think the young lady means flowers, your lordship.'

'Yes, sir. Thank you, sir. Flarze.'

'Oh?' said Lord Emsworth. 'Oh, flarze. Oh, ah, yes. I see.'

He looked worriedly round him at the gardens full of every kind of brightly coloured and sweet-smelling flower. There certainly were plenty of flarze in those gardens. But the problem was that Angus McAllister would go wild with anger if they were picked. The usual way of getting flowers out of McAllister was this – you waited until he was in a good mood, then you started a pleasant conversation with him, and then, choosing your moment carefully, you asked if he could possibly spare a few, to put in vases. The last thing you thought of doing was rushing into the garden and helping yourself.

'I – er . . .' said Lord Emsworth. He stopped. Suddenly he had seen himself clearly for what he was, a weak, worthless man who could not even make his employees obey him. The whole ancient line of Emsworths, from the first to the eighth earl, must be ashamed of him! Was he, the ninth Earl of Emsworth, going to let his fear of Angus McAllister prevent this delightful girl and her brother from getting all the flowers they needed? Or . . .

'Certainly, certainly, certainly,' he heard himself say. 'Take as many as you want.'

And so it happened that Angus McAllister saw a sight which first froze his blood and then made it boil. Running happily here and there through his perfect gardens, picking his perfect flowers, was a small girl. What made him even angrier was that it was the same small girl who, two days before, had hit him on the leg with a stone. The stillness of the summer evening was broken by a noise that sounded like a bomb exploding, as Angus McAllister rushed to the attack at sixty kilometres per hour.

Gladys quickly realized the danger she was in. She ran to where Lord Emsworth was standing, and hid behind him. The earl was not feeling so terribly good himself. We saw him at his bravest a few moments ago, but the truth is that when he decided to be brave, he thought McAllister was a safe kilometre away. His knees shook and his soul trembled within him.

And then something happened. It was, in itself, quite a small thing, but it had an enormous effect. Gladys put her small hot hand into Lord Emsworth's. It was a wordless vote of confidence, and it changed the situation completely. Lord Emsworth was suddenly filled with a cool masterfulness.

'Well, McAllister?' he said coldly.

He removed his top hat and brushed it against his coat.

'What is the matter, McAllister?'

He put his top hat back on his head.

'You appear annoyed, McAllister.' He threw his head back commandingly. The hat fell off. He let it lie on the ground. Free from it at last, he felt more masterful than ever.

'This young lady has my full permission to pick all the flowers she wants, McAllister. If you do not like this, say so, and we will discuss what you are going to do about it, McAllister. These gardens belong to me, McAllister, and if you do not – er – accept that fact, you will, no doubt, be able to find another employer – ah – more in agreement with your views. Er – dash it,' added his lordship, ruining the whole effect.

A long moment followed in which Nature stood still, holding her breath. Angus McAllister stared angrily at his employer. He had never imagined the earl would suggest he should find another job, and now that it had been suggested, Angus disliked the idea very much. Blandings Castle was in his bones. He would not feel happy anywhere else. He felt his beard, but it gave him no comfort.

He made his decision. Better to give up control, than to give up the Castle gardens.

'Mmhm,' said Angus McAllister.

'Oh, and by the way, McAllister,' said Lord Emsworth. 'About that gravel path. I've been considering it, and I won't have it. Ruin my beautiful grass with an ugly gravel path? Destroy one of the loveliest places in one of the finest and oldest

Gladys put her small hot hand into Lord Emsworth's.

gardens in the United Kingdom? Certainly not. Try to remember, McAllister, as you work in the gardens of Blandings Castle, that you are not back in Glasgow, working in the public parks. That is all, McAllister. Er – dash it – that is all.'

'Mmhm,' said Angus McAllister, in a low, defeated voice. He turned. He walked away. And Nature began to breathe again.

Lord Emsworth was shaken, but delighted. He had a new feeling of being a man among men. He almost wished – yes, dash it, he almost wished – that his sister Constance would come along and start giving him orders while he felt like this.

He had his wish.

'Clarence!'

Yes, there she was, hurrying towards him. She, like McAllister, seemed annoyed. Something was on her mind.

'Clarence!'

'Don't keep saying "Clarence!" like that,' said Lord Emsworth coldly. 'What the devil is the matter, Constance?'

'Matter? Do you know what the time is? Do you know that everybody is waiting down there for you to make your speech?'

Lord Emsworth looked her straight in the eye. 'I do not,' he said firmly. 'And I don't care. I'm not going to make any dashed speech. If you want a speech, make it yourself. Speech! I never heard such dashed nonsense in my life.' He turned to Gladys. 'Now, my dear,' he said, 'if you will just give me time to get out of these hellish clothes and this awful collar and put on something human, we'll go down to the village and spend some time with Ern.'

Trouble at Blandings

It was a beautiful afternoon. The sky was blue, the sun yellow, birds sang, and to cut a long story short, all Nature smiled. But Lord Emsworth's younger son Freddie Threepwood, as he sat in his car at the front door of Blandings Castle, with a fine big dog at his side, did not even notice these excellent weather conditions. He was thinking of dog biscuits.

Freddie was only an occasional visitor at the castle these days. Some years before, he had married the lovely daughter of Mr Donaldson of Donaldson's Dog-Delight, whose aim was to keep the American dog in top condition by providing it with health-giving biscuits. Freddie had gone to New York, to work for the company. He was in England now because Mr Donaldson had sent him to do what he could to encourage sales there. Aggie, his wife, had come with him, but after a week or so had found life at Blandings too quiet for her, and had left for the South of France. As soon as Freddie had finished his work in England, he planned to join her there.

Just then, a small, well-dressed gentleman of about sixty came down the front steps. This was Freddie's Uncle Galahad, a well-known figure at London theatres, restaurants, and music-halls, and at horse races all over the country. Freddie greeted him warmly. He knew that his Aunt Constance considered that Gally gave the family a bad name, but Freddie admired him as a man of endless resource and intelligence.

'Well, young Freddie,' said Gally. 'Where are you going with that dog?'

'I'm taking him to the Fanshawes, at Marling Hall.'

'That's where that pretty girl lives, isn't it? The one I met you with the other day?'

'That's right. Valerie Fanshawe. You see, her father keeps lots of dogs. And each one needs his daily biscuit. And what could be better for them than Donaldson's Dog-Delight?'

'You're going to sell him dog biscuits?'

'It'll be simple. He'll do anything for Valerie. She wants this dog and says that if I give it to her, she'll persuade the old man to send in a large order. I'm just going to deliver it.'

'But, my good Freddie, that is Aggie's dog. She'll be terribly angry if you give it away.'

'Don't worry, I've thought of that. I'll tell her it died, and I'll get her another one just as good. That'll keep Aggie quiet. But I must get on with things. See you later,' said Freddie, and disappeared in a cloud of smoke.

Gally shook his head. A lifetime of dancing, drinking and betting had made him the least narrow-minded of men, but he could not admire his nephew's way of doing business. Going back into the house, he met Beach, the butler. Beach was a little breathless, because he had been hurrying. Over the last few years he had become considerably heavier and slower; he was no longer the healthy young butler he had been when he first started work at the castle.

'This telegram has come for Mr Frederick, sir. I thought it might be important.'

'Most unlikely. Probably someone sending him the result of the four o'clock race somewhere. You've just missed him, anyway. Give it to me. I'll give it to him when he returns.'

Gally continued into the house, wondering how to pass the afternoon. He decided to go and talk to his brother Clarence, and found that gentle and dreamy lord in the smoking-room, staring fixedly at nothing.

'Ah, there you are, Clarence,' he said, and Lord Emsworth sat up with a jump, his whole body trembling.

'Oh, it's you, Galahad.'

'That's right. What's the matter, Clarence? A man whose soul is at rest does not jump out of his skin like that when somebody appears. Tell me all.'

A sympathetic listener was exactly what Lord Emsworth wanted. 'It's Connie,' he said unhappily. 'Did you hear what she was saying at breakfast?'

'I didn't come down to breakfast. I prefer to sleep late.'

'Ah, well, you missed it, then. Right in the middle of the meal – I was eating a fried egg at the time – she told me she was going to get rid of Beach.'

'What! Get rid of *Beach*!'

'"He is so slow," she said. "He gets breathless. We ought to have a younger, smarter butler." I was shocked. I nearly swallowed my fried egg whole.'

'I don't blame you. Blandings without Beach is unthinkable. So is Blandings with what she calls a younger, smarter butler. By Jove! I can imagine the sort of fellow she wants – some bright young man who will be running here, there and everywhere, and making us all feel old. You must show her who's boss, Clarence, and be firm.'

'Who, me?' said Lord Emsworth. What an idea! In name, of course, he was lord of Blandings, but in practice Connie's word was law. Look at the way she always made him wear a top hat at the Blandings Castle Open Day. Last time a child had even thrown a cake at it. But Connie always insisted.

'I can't be firm with Connie.'

'Well, I can, and I'm going to. Sack Beach, indeed! After eighteen years of service. It's a terrible idea. She must not be allowed to do this awful thing.'

At that moment, footsteps were heard in the hall and on the stairs. Lord Emsworth recognized them and looked even more unhappy. 'It's Frederick,' he said. He still felt that the less he saw of his younger son, the better.

'I've got a telegram for him,' said Gally, remembering. 'I'd better take it up to him.'

'Do,' said Lord Emsworth. 'And I think I'll go and have a

'*Mr Galahad and Mr Frederick fell downstairs.*'

look at my flowers.' But today, even his beautiful roses failed to cheer him up. The thought of Blandings without Beach simply ruined his ability to concentrate.

He was staring miserably at a flower-bed when Beach himself appeared. 'Excuse me, my lord. Mr Galahad asks if you would step inside to the smoking-room to speak to him.'

'Why can't he come out here?'

'He has hurt his ankle, my lord. He and Mr Frederick fell downstairs.'

'Oh?' Lord Emsworth was not particularly interested. Freddie was always doing strange things. So was Galahad. 'How did that happen?'

'It appears that Mr Galahad met Mr Frederick on the stairs and gave him a telegram. On reading it, Mr Frederick gave a surprised cry, and held on to Mr Galahad for support. Unfortunately, this sudden movement made them both fall downstairs. Mr Frederick, too, has hurt his ankle. He is in bed.'

When Lord Emsworth reached the smoking-room, he found Gally lying on a sofa, looking not greatly disturbed by his accident. He was smoking a cigar.

'Beach tells me you had a fall,' said Lord Emsworth. 'He seems to think it was something to do with Freddie's telegram.'

'That's right. It was from his wife.'

'Ah. Frances.'

'No, her name's Aggie. And you see, in it she says she will be arriving here the day after tomorrow.'

'I see no problem there.'

'Freddie does, and I'll tell you why. He's just given her dog to Valerie Fanshawe.'

'Who's Valerie Fanshawe?'

'You know, the daughter of Captain Fanshawe of Marling Hall. One of your neighbours. Haven't you met him?'

'No,' said Lord Emsworth, who never met anyone if he could help it. 'But why should Frances worry about Freddie giving this young woman a dog?'

'Aggie. And I didn't say *a* dog, I said *her* dog, whom she loves madly. It wouldn't matter so much if Valerie Fanshawe were fat, ugly and wore glasses, but unfortunately, she is a real beauty, with golden hair, blue eyes and a wonderful figure. As soon as Aggie sees Valerie Fanshawe and finds out that Freddie has given this lovely girl her favourite dog as a present, she'll probably divorce him. Wives often do that in America. And then her father will sack him, and he'll have to come back home.'

'What, to the castle?' cried Lord Emsworth, deeply shocked. 'My God!'

'So you see how serious the situation is. However, I've been giving it some deep thought, and I'm glad to say I've solved the problem. We must get that dog back before Aggie arrives here.'

'You will ask Rosalie Fanshawe to return it?'

'Valerie. No, she would refuse. Someone will have to steal it, and this is where you come in.'

'I?'

'Who else is there? Freddie and I are both lying on our beds of pain, unable to move, and I don't think we can ask Connie. Your quick intelligence has probably already told you what you have to do. Just walk around to the Fanshawes', say around ten o'clock tonight, and hide somewhere near the back door. Their butler is sure to let the dog out for its last visit to the bushes – everyone does that and it's always at the back door. And that's when you get hold of it and bring it back here.'

Lord Emsworth stared in horror. 'But, Galahad!'

'It's no good saying "But, Galahad!" It's got to be done. You don't want Freddie's whole future ruined, do you? Or to have him at the castle for the rest of his life? Ah, I see you tremble. And dash it, it's not much I'm asking of you. Just pick up a dog and bring it back. A child could do it.'

'But what if the dog refuses to come with me? After all, we haven't been introduced.'

'I've thought of that. You must put aniseed on your trouser legs. Dogs follow aniseed to the ends of the earth.'

'But I have no aniseed.'

'Beach will be able to find some. And Beach never asks questions. Unlike Connie's young, smart butler, who would probably be full of them.'

As Gally had said, Beach neither showed surprise at the request nor asked questions. He brought the aniseed, and at the appointed hour Lord Emsworth left for Marling Hall, smelling strongly. Gally lit another cigar, and started doing *The Times* crossword puzzle.

However, he found it difficult to concentrate on it. This was not only because these crossword puzzles had become so complicated recently, but because he seriously doubted whether his brother could carry out the plan successfully. There were so many possible ways in which he could fail, and he was famous for doing the wrong thing on every occasion.

Just then, heavy breathing was heard outside the door, and Beach entered, showing in an extremely good-looking young woman. 'Miss Valerie Fanshawe, sir,' he said.

'Oh, I'm sorry,' said Valerie. 'I really meant to see Freddie. You're his uncle, aren't you?'

'Yes, good evening. Do excuse me for not getting up. I've hurt my ankle. So has Freddie. He's in bed, by the way.'

The girl seemed puzzled. 'You've both hurt your ankles? What happened?'

'We fell downstairs together.'

'What made you do that?'

'Oh, we just thought we would. Can I give Freddie a message from you?'

'If you wouldn't mind. Tell him that Father *is* going to order *lots* of those dog biscuits.'

'Oh, that's excellent.'

'And I've brought back the dog.'

This was the most sensational piece of news. Gally sat straight up on the sofa. 'You've done *what*?' he cried.

'I've brought back the dog Freddie gave me. I'd love to keep it, but I can't. The stupid animal attacked and nearly killed Father's favourite dog, so he told me to get rid of it at once. Oh well. I do hope your ankle gets better soon. Goodbye.'

'What a wonderful piece of luck for Freddie,' thought Galahad. He was fond of Freddie, and to celebrate, he rang for Beach, to ask for a whisky. It was some considerable time before Beach arrived, breathless as usual.

'I'm very sorry to take so long, Mr Galahad. Captain Fanshawe was speaking to me on the telephone. He was asking for his lordship, but I have been unable to find him. It appears that the butler at Marling Hall caught someone hiding near the back door, obviously about to break into the house, and has locked him in the cellar. The captain wanted to warn us that there may be other thieves in the neighbourhood.'

This was a second piece of sensational news for Gally. He

had never imagined anything like this could happen, even to Clarence.

'Beach,' he said, 'prepare yourself for a shock. The supposed burglar who is now locked in the Fanshawe cellar is none other than Clarence, ninth Earl of Emsworth.'

'Sir!'

'I promise you, it's true. I sent him to Marling Hall, for a secret purpose, which must remain secret. How he managed to get caught, we shall never know. Now we have to get him out of that cellar. Don't speak. I must think, I must think.'

Such was Gally's intelligence that only a few moments passed before he was able to say, 'Beach! I've got it! You will have to go to Marling Hall and see the butler there. You know him well, and no doubt he will offer you a glass of something.' Gally then brought out a small bottle from his jacket pocket. 'You see this bottle, Beach? Sleeping pills. I always carry them with me. You never know when they'll be useful. Just put one of these into the butler's drink, and when you see him fall asleep, go and unlock the cellar door and bring his lordship home.'

'But, Mr Galahad! I really don't feel I can—'

'If, when the Fanshawes open up the cellar tomorrow morning, they find Clarence there, his good name will be lost. He'll never be able to show his face in the neighbourhood again. You can't let that happen. And another thing, Beach. Do this small thing for him, and he will be grateful to you for ever. Gold, palaces, jewels, you name it and it will be yours.'

The light of battle began to shine in Beach's eyes. 'Very good, Mr Galahad,' he said.

Gally continued with his crossword, on the sofa. About an hour later, Beach returned, to make his report to his commanding officer. The plan had worked beautifully, and Lord Emsworth was now safely back at Blandings Castle. Gally thanked Beach, and sent him off to bed.

Some minutes later, Lady Constance came angrily into the smoking-room. Gally was surprised. His sister did not often wish to talk to him.

'Oh, hullo, Connie,' he said. 'Are you any good at crossword puzzles?'

Lady Constance did not say, 'To hell with crossword

The plan had worked beautifully.

puzzles', but it was clear that she would have done if she hadn't been so well brought up.

'Galahad,' she said. 'Have you seen Beach? I have been ringing for him for half an hour. He really is getting far too old for his duties.'

'Clarence was telling me you were thinking of sacking him.'

'I am.'

'Well, I wouldn't if I were you.'

'What do you mean?'

'You'll be sorry if you do.'

'I don't understand you.'

'Then let me tell you a little bedtime story.'

'Please do not talk nonsense, Galahad. Really, I sometimes think you have less common sense than Clarence.'

'It is a story,' continued Gally, taking no notice, 'of a butler's love and service, far beyond the call of duty—'

'Have you been drinking, Galahad?'

'Only to the health of a butler who will be famous for centuries to come. Here is the story.'

He told it well, with all the details, and watched with interest as Lady Constance's face became paler and paler.

'So there you are,' said Gally, at the end. 'Even if you aren't touched by his selfless service, and lost in admiration at the way he puts sleeping pills in people's drinks, you must realize it would be madness to sack him. You can't afford to have him spreading the story of Clarence's evening activities all over the neighbourhood. If I were you, Connie, I would reconsider.'

He looked with pleasure at the ruin of what had once been a fine, masterful sister. He could read the message of that pale, shocked face, and could see that she was reconsidering.

GLOSSARY

* old-fashioned slang used mainly by the British upper classes

admire   to have a very good opinion of someone or something
ain't   *(ungrammatical)*   isn't, aren't
aniseed   strong-smelling plant seeds which attract dogs
bachelor   an unmarried man
bet *(v)*   to risk money on the result of something e.g. a race
biscuit   a flat, thin, dry cake
boy scout   a member of a special club for boys
brain   the part of our head that thinks, remembers, and feels
brainy   intelligent, clever
butler   the manservant in charge of running a large house
***by Jove!**   an exclamation of strong feeling
cannae *(Scots)*   cannot
career   work or a job for which special training is needed
***chap, chappie**   a man
check *(adj)*   a pattern made of crossed lines or squares of different
   colours
cosy   warm, comfortable, friendly
***dash it!**   an exclamation of annoyance
***dashed**   very (e.g. 'dashed interesting')
didn't have nothing *(ungrammatical)*   didn't have anything
earl   a title for a man of noble family
eyebrow   a line of short hairs above the eye
***fellow**   a man
fiancée   the woman whom a man is going to marry
firm *(adj)*   strong and determined in attitude and behaviour
gentleman   a man of good family, usually wealthy

giggle *(v)*   to laugh in a silly way

give up   to stop doing something

gravel   small stones often used to make a path

headmistress   the woman in charge of a school

hell   the worst place you can imagine; **hellish** *(adj)*

the Hon.   short for 'the Honourable', a title used for an earl's son

inebriated   of someone who has drunk too much alcohol

*jolly   happy, cheerful; very (e.g. 'jolly good')

jute   a plant used for making sacks and rope

kid *(slang)*   a child

liberty (take the liberty)   to dare to do something that is outside
   your area of responsibility

lift *(n)*   a free ride in a car, etc.

lord   a man of noble family; **your lordship**   words used when
   speaking to a lord

masterful   of someone who is good at deciding things and taking
   control

modest *(adj)*   not proud of yourself; **modesty** *(n)*

mule   an animal that is part horse and part donkey

music-hall   old-fashioned variety entertainment

notice (give notice)   to tell your employer that you will be leaving
   your job

*old thing   friendly words used when speaking to a close friend

portrait   a painting of a person

profile   a face seen from the side

publish   to print and sell books

pumpkin   a large, round, fleshy vegetable

put up with   to tolerate or bear

relieved *(adj)*   glad that a problem has gone away; **relief** *(n)*

reminiscences   memories of the past, often written

resource   the ability to think quickly and solve problems

***rummy**   strange, odd

sack *(v)*   to dismiss someone from a job

sigh *(v)*   to breathe out slowly, showing sadness, tiredness, etc.

smart   well dressed, clean, neat; *(esp. US)* clever

soul   the part of us that some people believe does not die

speech   a formal talk

stagger   to walk in an unsteady way; ***stagger**   to go, walk

stripe   a straight line of colour in a pattern

tact   knowing how and when to say things to avoid hurting people

telegram   a short, urgent message sent by electric current along wires, and then printed and delivered

telescope   a long instrument with special glass that makes distant things seem nearer

top hat   a man's tall hat with straight sides, only worn on formal occasions

twa *(Scots)*   two

valet   a gentleman's personal manservant

Jeeves and Friends

SHORT STORIES

ACTIVITIES

Before Reading

1 Read the story introduction on the first page of the book, and the back cover. What do you know now about the characters in these stories? Match the names with the descriptions.

Mr Bertram Wooster / Angus McAllister / the Earl of Emsworth / Jeeves / the Earl's sister Constance / the Earl's son Freddie

1 has difficulty remembering things
2 expects people to do what she tells them at once
3 has very poor dress sense and not much intelligence
4 gets involved with the wrong sort of girl
5 often gets angry, even with his employer, but is good at his job
6 is much more than just a servant

2 Read the story introduction again, and these quotes from the story. Can you guess who is speaking? Match the characters' names to the quotes.

Mr Bertram Wooster / Angus McAllister / the Earl of Emsworth / Jeeves / the Earl's sister Constance / the Earl's son Freddie

1 'Your lorrrdship will accept my notice.'
2 'Oh, about that check suit. Is it really awful?'
3 'I think I'll go and have a look at my flowers.'
4 'She's awfully intelligent, you know. You'll love her.'
5 'Do you know what the time is? Do you know that everybody is waiting down there for you to make your speech?'
6 'My plan is certain to succeed, sir.'

While Reading

Read *Jeeves Takes Charge*. Choose the best question-word for these questions, and then answer them.

What / Who / Why

1 . . . did Bertie sack his valet, Meadowes?
2 . . . was Bertie reading *Behavioural Types of Transactional Thinking*?
3 . . . looked wonderful when seen sideways, according to Bertie?
4 . . . was it important for Bertie and Florence to be pleasant to Uncle Willoughby?
5 . . . did Florence find so shocking about Uncle Willoughby's reminiscences?
6 . . . were thrown out of a music-hall in 1887?
7 . . . had Florence ordered Bertie to return to Easeby at once?
8 . . . did Bertie agree to do what Florence wanted?
9 . . . suggested searching Bertie's room for the parcel?
10 . . . posted the parcel to a London publisher?
11 . . . happened about Bertie's check suit in the end?

Read *The Artistic Career of Corky* down to the 'top hat' on page 23. Can you guess the answers to these questions?

1 Will Jeeves's plan work, exactly as intended?
2 Who will Muriel marry, and why?
3 What will happen to Corky's artistic career?
4 Who will inherit the Worple jute millions?
5 Will Bertie and Corky remain friends?

Read *Bertie Changes His Mind*. Are these sentences true (T) or false (F)? Rewrite the false sentences with the correct information.

1 Jeeves advises young valets to be imaginative and enthusiastic.
2 Jeeves hoped that Bertie would get married.
3 Bertie's plan was to go and live in India with his sister and her three little girls.
4 Jeeves hoped that a few days by the seaside would make Bertie forget about his plan.
5 Peggy Mainwaring was a rather sad, quiet, shy little girl.
6 Jeeves was not completely truthful in his conversation with Miss Tomlinson.
7 Bertie would have escaped before his talk if Jeeves hadn't pretended that the car had broken down.
8 Bertie knew that his talk had been a great success.
9 Jeeves made Bertie suffer in order to make him change his mind about living with small girls.

Read *Looking After the Pumpkin*. Who said this, and to whom? Who, or what, were they talking about?

1 'Perhaps if I removed the cover at the end of the telescope . . . '
2 'I've been meaning to tell you about that.'
3 'I cannae. She's paying me twa pounds a week for her food.'
4 'Speak! Tell me! Have the cats got at it?'
5 'Hi there! Stop that!'
6 '. . . my dear chap, do please tell the officer who I am.'
7 'Personally, I'm delighted. That boy is a fine young fellow.'
8 'Tell him – er – not to hurry home.'
9 'I didn't say I would. I was going to say "I will consider it".'
10 'See what you mean. Can't both win.'

Read *Lord Emsworth and the Girl Friend* down to the bottom of page 69. Can you guess what happens in the rest of the story? Circle Y (Yes) or N (No) for each of these possibilities.

1 Lord Emsworth makes sure that Gladys gets the best tea she has ever had. Y/N

2 Beach is sent to the village to ask Ern to the Castle for tea. Y/N

3 Ern is invited to pick as many flowers as he likes in the Castle gardens. Y/N

4 Lady Constance sends Gladys home, without any tea. Y/N

5 Gladys throws another stone at Angus McAllister. Y/N

6 Lord Emsworth tells Angus McAllister firmly that a gravel path is out of the question. Y/N

7 Angus McAllister resigns and goes to work for Sir Gregory Parsloe-Parsloe. Y/N

8 Lord Emsworth refuses to obey Constance's orders. Y/N

Read *Trouble at Blandings*, and then answer the questions.

1 Why had Freddie returned to England from New York?

2 Why did he give his wife's dog to Valerie Fanshawe, and what was Galahad's opinion of this?

3 What worrying news had Lord Emsworth heard at breakfast?

4 How did Galahad and Freddie hurt their ankles?

5 Who sent a telegram to Freddie, and what did it say?

6 Why was it important to get Aggie's dog back from Valerie Fanshawe, and why did Lord Emsworth agree to do it?

7 What went wrong with this plan, and why was it unnecessary anyway?

8 What did Beach do that was 'far beyond the call of duty'?

9 How did Galahad finally persuade Constance not to sack Beach?

After Reading

1 Here are some different titles for the stories. Which ones go with which stories? Which of the three is the best for each story? Why?

- A Bachelor Life is a Jolly One
- Beach Saves the Day
- An Uncle's Reminiscences
- Getting Rid of Freddie
- Jeeves and the Giggling Girls
- The Dog Biscuit Disaster
- The Birth of Baby Blobby
- The Open Day Hell
- Jeeves and the Bird Book

- The Prize Winner
- Educating Bertie
- Flowers for Gladys
- Taking a Liberty
- Valet to a Vegetable
- The Portrait Painter
- Sacking the Butler
- A Masterful Earl
- Jeeves and the Profile

2 Here are the thoughts of six characters (one from each story). Who is thinking, and what has just happened in each story?

1 'Poor Ern won't get anything nice for his tea now. Wonder where that nice old man is – said he'd be wearing a funny hat. Bet *he* wouldn't have put me in this 'orrible, dark shed . . .'

2 'How thoughtful of him to make that suggestion! We shall have the talk straight after tea. It will be most valuable for the girls to hear a few well-chosen words from a man of education and experience, someone they can all admire and look up to . . .'

3 'Oh really, that's the last straw! Where *is* the man? He's so slow these days! What *can* he be doing? He really will have to go. I'll try the smoking-room – Galahad might know where he is . . .'

4 'That was a quite unspeakably horrible evening! All those stories about my father! I'll have to put a stop to this book. Let me see . . . yes! It can be a little test for my foolish fiancé. I'll send him a telegram early tomorrow morning . . .'

5 'Mmhm. His lorrrdship is desperate for my return, is he? Well, that's as may be. He'll have to learn that he cannae speak to me like that. And his is not the only garrrden in the worrrld!'

6 'Who *is* this young lady? She's certainly an intelligent and sensitive writer! Very well-informed. I think I'll write and invite her to call on me. We could discuss my latest discovery about the eating habits of the Golden-winged Sunbird . . .'

3 **Which of these adjectives from the stories can be used to describe the characters? Make a list of adjectives that suit each character.**

aggressive, artistic, brainy, capable, cheerful, childish, fearless,
fierce, firm, foolish, forgetful, intelligent, masterful, modest,
motherly, purposeful, resourceful, selfless, sympathetic, tactful

Bertie Wooster	Jeeves	Lord Emsworth	Gladys
Lady Florence	Corky	Angus McAllister	Galahad
Miss Tomlinson	Mr Worple	Lady Constance	Beach

4 **Think about or discuss these questions. Use your lists of adjectives from above to help you discuss the characters.**

1 Which character or characters did you find funniest? Why?
2 Do you think the humour in these stories is mainly in the situations, or in the characters, or in the language?
3 Which was your favourite story, and why?

5 *Jeeves Takes Charge*

Perhaps Jeeves wrote to his aunt at the end of the story, to tell her about his new employer. Put the parts of sentences in the right order, and join them with the linking words to make a letter of six sentences. Start with number 5.

and / but / so / that / which / who

My dear aunt,

1 A day or two later Lady Florence broke off the engagement,

2 _____ his uncle was about to post to his publisher in London.

3 My new employer, Mr Wooster, is a very pleasant, if rather brainless, young gentleman,

4 _____ I soon managed to solve that little problem.

5 I am delighted to inform you

6 _____ has a most unfortunate liking for very loud suits.

7 This was clearly some kind of test for Mr Wooster,

8 _____ Mr Wooster is now extremely grateful to me for this.

9 He had also, most unwisely, got himself engaged to Lady Florence Craye,

10 _____ I took the parcel and posted it to the publisher myself.

11 Lady Florence had asked him to steal and destroy a book,

12 _____ I have found excellent employment through the agency.

With all good wishes from your dutiful nephew

6 *The Artistic Career of Corky*

At the end (page 31) Corky was 'most generous' to Jeeves. What did they both say? Complete Jeeves's side of the conversation.

CORKY: Jeeves, about that plan of yours – you knew what would happen when Muriel met my uncle, didn't you?

JEEVES: _____

CORKY: I was dashed miserable about losing her, I can tell you.

JEEVES: _____

CORKY: What do you mean, Jeeves? What was wrong with her?

JEEVES: _____

CORKY: Well, that's true. Artists can't afford expensive wives.

JEEVES: _____

CORKY: Maybe you're right, Jeeves. Well, all's well that ends well.

JEEVES: _____

CORKY: Doing very nicely, thank you, Jeeves. *The Sunday Star*
wants at least ten drawings a week for the next five years!

JEEVES: _____

CORKY: Thank you, Jeeves. But it's all because of you, you know.
Here you are . . . Have a drink or something on Baby Blobby!

7 **Bertie Changes His Mind**
**Here are Bertie's thoughts at the end of the story, as he sits in his
comfortable bachelor flat. Choose one suitable word for each gap.**

It's dashed cosy and _____ here, with old Jeeves _____ in with the
drinks _____ usual. Just imagine the _____ of having my sister's
_____ girls running around the _____! I must have been _____ even
to think about _____. Perhaps I was still _____ weak after my
recent _____. Well, that's what Jeeves _____, and he knows. If
_____ is one thing I've _____ from this, it's that _____ is always
right! That _____ experience today! I had _____ idea small girls
could _____ like that – they just _____ stopped! And having to
_____ a talk to hundreds _____ them was enough to _____ a fellow
to death! _____ Jeeves hadn't repaired the _____ in time, who
knows _____ Miss Tomlinson would have _____ to me! He's a
_____ in a million. How _____ I've got him to _____ after me!
Might have _____ glass of brandy, to celebrate.

8 *Looking After the Pumpkin*
Imagine you are a Shrewsbury reporter, writing a report about the
pumpkin prize at the Agricultural Show. Use the notes below, and
try to include these three quotes if possible.

Sir Gregory Parsloe-Parsloe: '*I must confess it was a disappointment
to me. But may the best man win, don't you know!*'
Angus McAllister: '*The pumpkin and I understand each other. I know
how it feels – it cannae be bothered with talking, same as me.*'
Clarence, Earl of Emsworth: '*You know, I love that pumpkin like a
son! Well, to be absolutely truthful,* more *than a son.*'

• winner / biggest pumpkin / ninth Earl of Emsworth / Blandings
  Castle / head-gardener / understands pumpkins
• younger son, the Hon. Freddie / recently married / American
  millionaire's daughter / now sells dog biscuits / USA
• Lord Emsworth / delighted / son working / New York / strange /
  not yet met / son's bride
• Lord Emsworth / worrying time / head-gardener / recently
  sacked / disagreement / back in service / double the salary
• story / Lord Emsworth / arrested / roses / London park
• Sir Gregory Parsloe-Parsloe / pumpkin prize / last three years
• pumpkin / largest seen / Shrewsbury / many years

9 *Lord Emsworth and the Girl Friend*
At the end, after Lord Emsworth had gone down to the village with
Gladys, perhaps Lady Constance asked Beach what had been going
on. Complete Beach's side of the conversation.

LADY CONSTANCE: Beach, what exactly has Clarence been doing
    this afternoon? Do you know?
BEACH: _____

LADY CONSTANCE: Tea? With that little London girl? Really! And
what was in that basket the girl was carrying?

BEACH: _____

LADY CONSTANCE: Oh, Clarence is hopeless! That boy bit my leg,
you know, Beach.

BEACH: _____

LADY CONSTANCE: It wasn't a deep wound, fortunately. But never
mind that now. Where did the girl get all those flowers from?

BEACH: _____

LADY CONSTANCE: What! You mean Clarence gave her permission
to pick them? No wonder McAllister was so angry!

BEACH: _____

LADY CONSTANCE: Why, whatever else could there be?

BEACH: _____

LADY CONSTANCE: No gravel path? Clarence told McAllister that?
To his face? I simply don't understand what's come over him!

10 *Trouble at Blandings*

Galahad told his sister Constance the story of Clarence's rescue
from the Fanshawes' cellar (see page 85). Complete the sentences in
as many words as you like, to finish Galahad's story.

Once upon a time there was a charming young man called Freddie,
who married _____. Young Freddie, although not very
clever, was ambitious, and one day, as part of his business plan
_____. Suddenly a telegram was received at the castle
_____. At once Freddie's father was sent to the neighbours'
house _____.

Fortunately, a man of great bravery and intelligence appeared
_____. Yes, I am speaking of Beach, _____.

ABOUT THE AUTHOR

Pelham Grenville Wodehouse (pronounced Woodhouse), or Plum, as he was known to his family and friends, was born in 1881 in Guildford, in the south of England. He started his writing career in 1900, while still at school, and although he began working as a bank clerk, he resigned in 1903 to become a full-time writer and journalist. He published his first novel when he was twenty-one, and went on to establish himself as a humorous writer with titles such as *Psmith in the City* (1910), *Piccadilly Jim* (1918), and *The Man with Two Left Feet* (1917) – the collection of stories that first introduced Bertie Wooster and his famous 'gentleman's gentleman', Jeeves.

Wodehouse wrote nearly 100 novels and almost 300 short stories. He spent a lot of time in New York, where he wrote song lyrics for successful musical comedies with Cole Porter, Irving Berlin, and George Gershwin. He also wrote plays for the theatre, and film scripts for Hollywood in the 1930s. After the Second World War he and his wife settled in the USA, and in 1955 he became an American citizen. He died in 1975 on Long Island, near New York, at the age of ninety-three.

P. G. Wodehouse became one of the most popular humorists of his time, and is still regarded as a comic genius today. His admirers have formed Wodehouse appreciation societies in many countries, and his work is often adapted for television and the cinema. His stories, with their light touch and kind-hearted humour, have given pleasure to countless readers. Wodehouse himself described his writing as 'making a sort of musical comedy without music and ignoring real life altogether.'

ABOUT BOOKWORMS

OXFORD BOOKWORMS LIBRARY
Classics • True Stories • Fantasy & Horror • Human Interest
Crime & Mystery • Thriller & Adventure

The OXFORD BOOKWORMS LIBRARY offers a wide range of original and adapted stories, both classic and modern, which take learners from elementary to advanced level through six carefully graded language stages:

Stage 1 (400 headwords)	**Stage 4** (1400 headwords)
Stage 2 (700 headwords)	**Stage 5** (1800 headwords)
Stage 3 (1000 headwords)	**Stage 6** (2500 headwords)

More than fifty titles are also available on cassette, and there are many titles at Stages 1 to 4 which are specially recommended for younger learners. In addition to the introductions and activities in each Bookworm, resource material includes photocopiable test worksheets and Teacher's Handbooks, which contain advice on running a class library and using cassettes, and the answers for the activities in the books.

Several other series are linked to the OXFORD BOOKWORMS LIBRARY. They range from highly illustrated readers for young learners, to playscripts, non-fiction readers, and unsimplified texts for advanced learners.

Oxford Bookworms Starters   *Oxford Bookworms Factfiles*
Oxford Bookworms Playscripts   *Oxford Bookworms Collection*

Details of these series and a full list of all titles in the OXFORD BOOKWORMS LIBRARY can be found in the *Oxford English* catalogues. A selection of titles from the OXFORD BOOKWORMS LIBRARY can be found on the next pages.

Three Men in a Boat

JEROME K. JEROME

Retold by Diane Mowat

'I like work. I find it interesting . . . I can sit and look at it for hours.'

With ideas like this, perhaps it is not a good idea to spend a holiday taking a boat trip up the River Thames. But this is what the three friends – and Montmorency the dog – decide to do. It is the sort of holiday that is fun to remember afterwards, but not so much fun to wake up to early on a cold, wet morning.

This famous book has made people laugh all over the world for a hundred years . . . and they are still laughing.

Cranford

ELIZABETH GASKELL

Retold by Kate Mattock

Life in the small English town of Cranford seems very quiet and peaceful. The ladies of Cranford lead tidy, regular lives. They make their visits between the hours of twelve and three, give little evening parties, and worry about their maid-servants. But life is not always smooth – there are little arguments and jealousies, sudden deaths and unexpected marriages . . .

Mrs Gaskell's timeless picture of small-town life in the first half of the nineteenth century has delighted readers for nearly 150 years.

The Garden Party and Other Stories

KATHERINE MANSFIELD

Retold by Rosalie Kerr

Oh, how delightful it is to fall in love for the first time! How exciting to go to your first dance when you are a girl of eighteen! But life can also be hard and cruel, if you are young and inexperienced and travelling alone across Europe . . . or if you are a child from the wrong social class . . . or a singer without work and the rent to be paid.

Set in Europe and New Zealand, these nine stories by Katherine Mansfield dig deep beneath the appearances of life to show us the causes of human happiness and despair.

Pride and Prejudice

JANE AUSTEN

Retold by Clare West

'The moment I first met you, I noticed your pride, your sense of superiority, and your selfish disdain for the feelings of others. You are the last man in the world whom I could ever be persuaded to marry,' said Elizabeth Bennet.

And so Elizabeth rejects the proud Mr Darcy. Can nothing overcome her prejudice against him? And what of the other Bennet girls – their fortunes, and misfortunes, in the business of getting husbands?

This famous novel by Jane Austen is full of wise and humorous observation of the people and manners of her times.

Cold Comfort Farm

STELLA GIBBONS

Retold by Clare West

The farm lies in the shadow of a hill, and the farmyard rarely sees the sun, even in summer, when the sukebind hangs heavy in the branches. Here live the Starkadders – Aunt Ada Doom, Judith, Amos, Seth, Reuben, Elfine . . . They lead messy, untidy lives, full of dark thoughts, moody silences, and sudden noisy quarrels.

That is, until their attractive young cousin arrives from London. Neat, sensible, efficient, Flora Poste cannot *bear* messes (they are so *uncivilized*). She begins to tidy up the Starkadders' lives at once . . .

Decline and Fall

EVELYN WAUGH

Retold by Clare West

After a wild, drunken party, Paul Pennyfeather is forced to leave Oxford and begin a new life out in the wide world. His experiences take him from a boys' private school in Wales, where he meets some rather strange people, to a life of luxury in a grand country house and the Ritz Hotel, and then to seven years' hard labour in prison. Where will it all end?

The black humour of this story about English society in the 1920s is as fresh today as it was when the novel was first written.